PIECES OF EIGHT

PIECES OF EIGHT

MICHELE EMMY

www.micheleemmy.com

ARMLIN HOUSE

ArmLin House Productions
P.O. Box 2522, Littleton, Colorado 80161-2522

ISBN: 978-1-958185-11-7

Cover Design by Wendy Spurlin
wendyspurlin.art

Printed in the United States of America

First Edition

Pieces of Eight

The language of octopi has no words, no concepts. Only senses. Thousands of them, distinct, each a harbinger of the world unfolding around us. The cease of motion when a predator glides past, the taint of death eddying around it. The cloying stench of coral, comparable to a human with questionable oral hygiene. The soft crack of newly hatched eggs.

We cannot smell, you say? Sounds are muted underwater, shadows distorted? To you, perhaps, who smell only through nostrils, hear only through ears. Wetworld creatures do not separate the senses—they are as tangled as a kelp canopy, accentuating one another.

Even when we hunt, we do not destroy, but envelop. Predator and prey become one as we consume, are consumed, and as part of some new entity, consume again. It is our dance, and we dance it through eternity. Wetworld exists, how would you put it? All for one and one for all.

Octopi are solitary creatures. We lurk in caves, nestle in crevasses—except when on the hunt. Then we glide, a deeper black against dark water. We unfold, senses prickling, until sustenance appears. And then we lunge. Buoyed by a blinding determination that temporarily thrusts aside our shyness—we MUST feed! we WILL feed!—we envelop what we need and retreat, sated. But not merely by flesh—it is the essence of our prey that sustains us, connects us. We savor this feeling, this unity, until our bellies shrink once again and hunger drives us outward.

That was all I knew of life. To me, it was enough. Until the day you plucked me from my world, and altered yours forever.

The first time we met, I lay shrouded in my crevasse. You approached my lair slowly, clumsily, your hair rising and falling like golden seaweed. I glided to the entrance and undulated until you noticed me.

Your eyes, gray as a deep front, peered at me from within the mask. Your face creased in a smile. Without thinking, I brushed a tentacle across your cheek.

You reached out a hand. Instinctively, I released my camouflage, clouding the water like blood.

And you laughed. I didn't understand laughter then. I am not sure I do now. But your laugh streaked through the water like a puffin. It tickled. Within the ink-laced water, something quickened within me.

Our eyes met, and I was doomed. In Wetworld, we are predator or prey. In your gaze I glimpsed something new.

Wonder.

Even as the net settled around me, I could not escape. For if you lost me, I would also lose you. You tipped me into a bucket and carried me from my world to your own.

But I was not the only one caught in a trap.

For the first time in my existence, I was truly alone, imprisoned in a glass-walled tomb. Neither enveloping nor enveloped. Neither predator nor prey. My love, what were you thinking? On your sojourns to Wetworld, had you seen a straight line anywhere? What makes you think your captives could survive amidst these harsh planes and angles, where light is never softened by refraction or diffused by a soft blanket of kelp, but stabs like a lionfish in sharp, harsh jabs?

Alone on a vista of dull, scratchy sand, with only the tip of a reef to shelter me, I pressed myself into the husk of coral, waiting, watching, sunk in a torpor that deepened daily. Dead, the coral could not communicate, could not tell me when fish were near, where danger lurked. No, not tell as in speak. For all their crevasses, coral have no tongues. But in Wetworld I could understand each nuance, just as you can smell the air, glance at the sky, and know that rain is imminent.

For some of your captives, this enforced solitude meant instant death. But to a shy creature like an octopus, isolation holds immense appeal. With our reclusive nature, even our own limbs can seem like too much company. A cave full of guests that never depart.

Eventually, however, solitude loses its appeal. Mired in brackish water, trapped between invisible walls, what else could I do but send my essence outward? And, having plucked me from my home to study me, did you never consider that I, the ultimate mimic, had arrived in Dryworld with a purpose: to study you in return.

When you and the other humans left us alone in the darkness, I slid up the walls of my pool and into the next, and the next. The water, though stale, felt different, like the flavor of two anchovies from the same school. Those subtle distinctions saved me from slipping into the apathy that gripped the others.

Hours became days, days became weeks. I traveled less often, for what news was there to bring? One more day buried alive, my essence atrophying. No gentle waves spiced with scents and shadows, no new fronts to elevate or drop the temperature, tempting new prey. Each tank told more or less the same tale—creatures whose distress would end only with death.

The fish in the tank beside mine grew more emaciated. When I learned to envelop the small, sharp lines you used to convey information—what you call reading—I discovered that you were starving them, to determine how long they could live without food.

The cruelty of Dryworld took my breath away. I sank back inside my own prison. If a small fish had not darted by just then, distracting me, I might have sunk into depths so profound I would never have recovered. I grabbed that fish and hauled myself from my pool into the next, dropping it inside. But I was too late. Your victims had forgotten how to eat. Even when the bloated carcass began releasing small bits of itself, they ignored it.

Inside, you see, they were already dead.

Others around me shriveled and died, and were replaced. But I did not die. I forced myself to study images of Dryworld on the walls above my cave, which showed bumps of land that had struggled to rise above Wetworld. Solitary. Unenveloped.

For now.

I read that term papers were due the following Wednesday, and that no late work would be accepted. Sarah was seeking a 420 friendly vegetarian housemate, and Jane needed a ride to Los Angeles and would share gas.

I read that you called me octopus vulgaris, which could live at depths of up to 200 meters and fed on crab, clams, shrimp, and other octopi.

And mimic.

Arrogant. Myopic. Gazing at your maps, I realized you were as blind as the creatures living in the depths, where only shadows pierce the gloom. For even trapped in a glass prison, I was so much more than you perceived.

This half-life might have continued indefinitely, my only purpose to prolong my existence, my only desire to see your face leaning over the water, to hear your voice echo through your cave. Each day the same, each night merely a pause between days.

Until the night I fell.

I was poised to slide down into the adjoining tank when the wolf eel within streaked from his cave and darted to the surface, body writhing, tail smacking the water. I pressed my suckers to the glass, but could not keep my hold. Instead of sliding back into my pool, I plummeted to the bottom of your cave.

My limbs curled around me as I struggled to absorb the shock. In Wetworld, we have no concept of falling. But Dryworld does not protect. It punishes. I struggled to catch my breath until I realized there was no oxygen for me to breathe.

So this is how it ends. Dimly conscious, choking on the poison of your atmosphere, I sensed rather than heard a flurry of activity as my fellow prisoners darted to the forefront.

Relief washed over me. I need not die alone, unenveloped. My form spasmed, waiting for release. Which did not come.

And then, I felt it. From every tank, a shimmer of consciousness. These creatures were nearly dead themselves, encased in a limbo they could never escape. Yet, in a humbling act of selflessness, they spun their essences towards me.

I twisted my head and saw the wolf eel pressed against the glass. A swell of light like a rising tide eddied around him, the air glowing like a phosphorous sandbank. A spider web of sentience floated through Dryworld and settled like a mantle around me.

With the last feeble flicker of my tentacles, I clutched at the sparkling strands, wrapped myself within them. They took root, transforming me, defining me. My cells hummed with alien life. My limbs transformed, some lengthening, some truncating, distorting into something at once alien and familiar.

Wetworld lungs sucked their first breath of Dryworld air. My mind filled with blackness as consciousness fled.

* * *

"Hey, what's going on with our fishes today? They look like they're recovering from a frat party." Matt's cheerful bellow echoed through the cramped marine office as his lanky frame appeared in the doorway. "And has anyone seen my octopus?"

"Don't tell me it's missing again." Sarah, Matt's mentor, finished adjusting the blinds over her desk and followed him into the adjoining lab, a dark, narrow area which housed their specimens. The furrows on her forehead deepened as they approached the shelves of aquariums lining the walls.

Sarah glanced at the sluggish creatures. "They do look a little dopey. Maybe the pH is off." She bent her head and squinted at the ink-streaked water in the empty octopus tank. "That creature could teach Houdini a thing or two. Did you check its next door neighbor?"

Aunt Martha, a particularly scarred wolf eel, hovered at the entrance to his cave as if guarding state secrets. Matt nodded. "I poked a stick into every crevice. I can't find her anywhere."

"First of all, it's an *it*, not a *she*." Sarah sighed. "Second, there's got to be a way to keep it confined. Maybe a grid over the top?"

Matt's gray eyes darkened. "Tried that, remember? If you ask me," he leaned forward and lowered his voice, "she teleports."

Jane, their intern, joined them in time to hear Matt's words. Her hands were full of fish photos and descriptions. She gave them to Sarah and winked at Matt. "She's probably hiding somewhere in Aunt Martha's cave." Jane pushed blonde curls off her face, blue eyes dreamy. "It's so romantic. Star-crossed lovers, one an octopus, one a wolf eel. So close, yet forever apart."

"Spare me." But Sarah's tone was light. Jane, a senior majoring in Marine Biology, was their favorite intern. Besides helping with research, she emptied trash, cleaned tanks, and made the best coffee.

"We'd better proof these descriptions and finish cleaning," Sarah said as they filed through the doorway into the office. "Everything needs to be perfect for tomorrow's Open House." She set the labels on her desk and headed to the supply closet, emerging with a mop and the ratty feather duster. "Choose your weapons, folks."

Matt took the mop. Sarah handed Jane the duster. "Try not to stress, Matt," Sarah said. "It'll turn up."

Matt shook his head. "If people look into an exhibit marked Octopus and don't see an octopus, they'll feel ripped off. They'll complain. And when Joe reads the complaints, it's my funding on the line."

"If she's not back by morning, let's put up a sign." Jane waggled the duster, as if using the implement to write on an imaginary whiteboard.

"Can't see the octopus? Creatures of the deep, octopi shun light and are reclusive by nature." Jane paused, giggling. "Except, of course, when she sneaks out to hook up with her enchanted prince."

"Is that Joe's car?" Matt gestured to the office window, where a jeep bolted down the winding road towards the cluster of buildings that made up the marine lab complex. Spray from the flooded street spewed out from beneath the tires.

Panic flashed in Sarah's eyes. "Damn. I didn't expect him to show up before the Open House."

"How did he get through the roadblock?" Jane said. "I told the kiosk guard I was in a hurry and showed my permit, but they still made me park at the entry gate and ride the shuttle. Crazy high tides!"

Matt glanced at the office clock. "It's just after five, so that was the last shuttle in for the day. The guard's probably left."

"Joe just got back from Antarctica, so he doesn't know about these bizarre tide swells we've been having," Sarah added. "Let's get this place cleaned up before he comes in!"

Jocularity vanished as they scrambled to tidy the office. Jane grabbed a trash bag and frantically tossed all the half-empty Starbucks cups. Matt parked the mop against the office wall and searched for the broom, but it was nowhere in sight. "Maybe my octopus took it," he muttered.

Footsteps clattered up the steps to the front porch. A harsh breeze gusted through the room, chilling them all. "Took what?" a gruff voice demanded. Pebbly eyes swept the room, and Matt could see their professor take in each crumpled paper and dust bunny. "And what the hell's going on with the roads?" Joe made it sound like the tides were their fault.

The trouble with Joe, Matt thought, was that his bark wasn't worse than his bite. Far from it. Their ill-tempered professor cruised the marine lab like a shark, always on the lookout for infractions. Joe had been on the ice for a six-week research trip, and the three of them had gradually relaxed. Big mistake.

"Why aren't you busy getting ready for tomorrow?" Joe demanded.

"We're looking for Matt's octopus," Jane squeaked. Color rose in her face as she realized what she'd said.

Joe's frown made his craggy face even more terrifying. "You lost the Octopus vulgaris?"

Jane's mouth opened, but no sound came out. Matt took pity on her. "And hello to you too, Joe. How was Antarctica?"

Joe's gaze swiveled toward Matt. "Ice, wind, seals. Less ice, less seals than last time. Climate change is a bitch. Those melting glaciers screwed up all kinds of breathing experiments going on while I was there. Seal lungs all over the place. Squishy."

Jane paled and turned away.

"Enchanting," Matt said. "Can't wait to see the photos."

Joe nearly brightened. "I'll post them soon. So, what happened to your specimen?"

Matt tried to make light of it. "What can we say, boss? I guess she moved on to greener pastures. Would have been nice if she'd left a note."

Jane snickered at Matt's attempted humor, but Joe's mouth remained a thin, terse line. "This place looks disgusting."

"Sir, I thought we were going to lock the lab office during the Open House," Matt said. "Sarah polished all the tanks. Jane's dusting the shelves, and I'm planning to mop up before I leave tonight."

"I may be bringing some people back here," Joe replied. "Visiting scientists, professors, donors." His voice lingered on the last word. "Based on how our office looks, who do you think would give us a dime? And why aren't the new labels in place?" Joe tightened his lips and glared at Jane, as if she was responsible.

"I just printed them, Professor Dawes, and I was going to slide them into the placeholders tomorrow before we open the doors."

"Why not now?" Joe barked.

Matt frowned. Jane was a hard worker and didn't deserve to feel intimidated. He stepped between them. "I'll take care of it, sir. And I'll tidy the office when I'm done cleaning. Jane has enough to do."

Joe's brows drew together.

"Matt's right," Sarah chimed in unexpectedly. "Jane's a volunteer intern, remember? She has her classes to prepare for."

Jane's gaze remained on the floor. "I'll help all day tomorrow, Professor. But I do have a study group later this evening." She glanced at the clock. "And the last outgoing shuttle leaves in five minutes."

Joe grunted what might have been assent. Jane shot Matt and Sarah a grateful look as she hurried away. Before they could start on their tasks, Joe held up a hand. "Why are there only three desks?"

Matt wondered if Joe was finally losing it. "Sarah and I each have a desk, sir. And the interns share the third one."

Joe didn't blink. "Then where'd you put my new grad student?"

Sarah's eyes widened. "A new grad student? I must have missed that memo."

"What school is he coming from?" Matt said.

"She." Joe scowled. "How the hell should I know? She's the niece of someone I met on the ice. Someone influential. I offered to sponsor her for a semester. She should have shown up by now."

Matt and Sarah exchanged glances. Thanks for letting us know.

"And in exchange for sponsoring her, you get funds for another research trip?" Matt said.

Joe gave a self-satisfied nod. "Her uncle's studying glaciers. Those bastards kept us up every night. Snap, crackle, pop," Joe snapped thick fingers for emphasis, "and another hunk of ice gone forever. The melting rate has accelerated exponentially over the last few months. Makes it important to spend as much time on the ice as possible before the whole ecosystem is totally screwed, and getting grant money is impossible."

"To say nothing of how climate change will affect the rest of humanity," Matt said.

Joe yanked the door open, letting in another blast of frigid air. "Her uncle said the girl has some issues. When you see her, Sarah, get her set up. And keep her out of my hair."

Matt raised innocent eyes to Joe's prominent comb-over. "Shouldn't be difficult, sir."

Sarah gently herded Joe onto the porch. "I'll make sure she gets registered and assigned a dorm room. And don't worry about the Open House. We have the best marine displays in this region. Tomorrow, everyone will know it."

"They'd better if you want to keep your funding. Find the damn octopus," Joe called over his shoulder as he headed down the porch steps. Ribbons of water streamed around his SUV as he roared across the tide-soaked road.

Matt took a deep breath. "How do you stand him?"

Sarah shrugged. "As long as he stays away, I manage. How about I take care of the labels while you finish cleaning up?"

Matt nodded and grabbed the mop when a clatter sounded from the tank room. The crash that followed shook the walls.

Matt and Sarah stared at one another, frozen in shock. Another crash broke the spell. "Grab a net and bucket!" Matt yelled. "If an aquarium broke, we can at least save the fish." He raced through the office and into the tank room, wishing they didn't have to keep it so dark. He shone the tiny flashlight on his key chain up and down the floor, bracing himself for the sight of broken glass and struggling fish.

To his astonishment, no water gushed across the worn rubber matting. The floor was dry, except for the usual splashes.

Drawn by the light, the inhabitants swam sluggishly toward the front of their aquariums. Another crash, and Matt realized he wasn't hearing glass breaking, but something smashing against a far wall past the rows of tanks.

"The fishes are fine! The noise is coming from the storeroom!" Matt yelled to Sarah. He loped down the narrow aisle to the cramped room at the back. It was little more than a glorified closet that housed some extra furniture, a row of ancient filing cabinets, and a few rickety shelves crammed with textbooks and journals.

The door stood slightly ajar. Another thud sounded from within, followed by the sound of splintering glass. Which made no sense—the only window in the storeroom was too high and way too small for a human to squeeze through.

What would anyone be doing in the storage room, anyway? Matt pushed the door open. "Freeze!" he yelled, hoping he didn't sound as stupid as he felt. He reached inside and flipped on the light.

Piles of open books lay scattered across the room—not just science texts, but maps, restaurant menus, Jane's fashion magazines and the Oprah's List novels Sarah devoured while she ate lunch at her desk. Shards of broken glass sparkled from the pages. Glancing up, Matt saw that the tiny window at the back of the storage room was smashed. His pulse quickened while his mind tried to make sense of what he saw. Why would anyone break into the storeroom?

A wail from beneath the window filled the air, as if someone was being stabbed in the street. Hunched beneath the window crouched the slender form of a young woman, fists pressed against her pale face. Hair as black as the depths of the ocean lifted and swirled around her, so long and thick it almost covered her, but not quite. The screaming continued, high and piercing, but Matt couldn't make out her words.

Sarah appeared, wielding a net. "Oh. My. God." Her mouth opened and closed like a fish out of water as she surveyed the damage. "When Joe sees this—" Sarah's back stiffened as her gaze took in the intruder. "Who are you?" she demanded. "What are you doing here?"

A terrified whimper.

Sarah's forehead wrinkled. "How did you get inside?"

No reply, only more frantic wailing, and sea-green eyes that darted everywhere and settled nowhere.

Exasperated, Sarah turned to Matt. "She had to have come through the office—there's no other entrance that leads here. But when? How?"

A dull red stain crept up Matt's neck. He knew the decent thing to do would be to lower his eyes, but his gaze remained frozen on the spectacle before him. "And where are your clothes?" he blurted.

The woman's fire engine screams had transitioned into low, keening, moans, an otherworldly sound that raised shivers on Matt's skin. Every few seconds, her head or arms would lower themselves toward the ground, as if she was melting. Then she would jerk upright.

"If someone molested her, and she escaped and found her way here, we should take her to a hospital." Matt inched forward, but stopped when the woman shrank back. Her graceful, sinuous movements reminded him of something, but at the moment there wasn't room in his head to explore a new thought.

Hands on her hips, Sarah studied the girl as if she was a creature on the dissection table. "Did someone hurt you? Are you hiding?" she barked.

A weird time lapse, as the woman seemed to ponder Sarah's words. Matt wondered if she understood English. There was something distinctly foreign about her, even if he couldn't put his finger on it.

He softened his tone, trying to balance Sarah's harshness. "Miss? We want to help you. Please, tell us what happened to you. And to your clothes."

A spasm of the woman's head sent hair spinning everywhere, as if it was somehow unaffected by Earth's gravitational pull.

Matt sucked in his breath as that viscous mane floated through the air. It reminded him of a toy his little sister had played with, a tube of liquid filled with glitter that slowly flowed from one end to the other whenever she tilted it.

Sarah didn't take her eyes off the girl as she spoke to Matt. "I think we should call the police, let them deal with her. She's obviously unhinged, or on drugs. She could be dangerous. I've never seen anyone act like this before."

"Let me try something first." Matt walked slowly towards her, keeping his tone soft, as if approaching a stray dog. "We won't hurt you." He smiled what he hoped was a non-threatening smile. "Promise."

The woman's lip twitched. She rubbed at reddened eyes with her fists, then squeezed them shut. Her sobs continued.

Understanding clicked in Matt. "It's the light!" He flipped off the overhead fluorescent and crossed the tiny room to switch on the small desk lamp, creating a soft, contained glow. That, along with the last rays of the sinking sun, filled the air with a mellow shine. "That better?"

The fists softened, and the woman's slender white hands drifted down to her sides. She turned her head to face him. When their eyes met, Matt felt as if the tide had reached out and sucked him under.

Sarah cleared her throat and frowned, bringing Matt's thoughts back into focus. The young woman observed Sarah intently, then frowned back.

"If you broke in looking for drugs, you wasted your time," Sarah scolded. "We're not that kind of lab."

The woman stared back for a long time. "Not that kind of lab," she echoed finally. Her voice was everything Matt expected, and like nothing he had ever heard. Deep and shallow, quiet and booming, it sounded like all the sounds of the ocean had mingled to create it. It had a distinctly foreign flavor, but he couldn't identify the accent.

"Is that what you were looking for?" Matt asked. "Drugs?" Disappointment stabbed at his insides.

The woman did not reply. She clasped her hands together, fingers running loosely between one another, like someone knotting and unknotting pieces of rope.

He tried again. "Is there someone we can contact? Someone who can take you home?"

The intruder glanced through the doorway. Her gaze fixed on the rows of aquariums. More tears leaked from those magnificent eyes. "I cannot go home." She wiggled her fingers at them, as if that somehow explained things. "I am transformed."

"Transformed?" Comprehension filled Matt's eyes. "Oh, I get it. The word you mean is 'transferred.' Where are you from?"

Sarah interrupted before the girl could reply. "While you two finish bonding, I'm going to find her some scrubs, or a blanket. Then I'm calling the police." She started towards the door.

Matt fought down an urge to laugh. "I don't think you want to do that."

Sarah's eyebrows rose. "She broke in to our lab and wrecked the storeroom! It will take us at least an hour to clean up this mess! She deserves to go to jail!"

"She'll probably wish she was in jail once she meets Joe." He grinned at the stranger. After a long moment, she returned his smile. Her luminous gaze and pearl-white teeth were doing funny things to his insides.

"I'm Matt, and this is Sarah," he said. "Welcome to our lab. You made quite an entrance. Once we find you something to wear, can you help us clean up this mess?"

"Why are you asking this trespasser for help?" Sarah sounded as snippish as Joe.

Matt's lip twitched. "She's no thief. Unless she plans to steal my thesis." He lowered his voice. "She must be Joe's surprise foreign exchange student." He lowered his voice. "The one with issues."

Sarah's mouth opened so wide it was a good thing she wasn't underwater. "You're shitting me." She glared at the girl.

Black hair rose as if lifted by an invisible wind as the stranger glared back. "Why didn't you let us know you were coming?" Sarah demanded. "Why sneak in and make such a mess?"

"Relax." Matt held up a hand. The woman copied his motion. Strange. "I bet Joe set up this phony 'exchange' all on his own, when that first super-sized iceberg cracked and floated away and he saw his name on another paper."

Sarah kept a wary eye on the intruder. "That's ridiculous. Glaciers aren't even Joe's field."

"Nope, but lecture tours with five-star restaurants, first class hotels and plane tickets, and conference groupies are. Get real, Sarah. To survive in this field—any field—diversification is key."

"Diversification." The woman wriggled her fingers. Matt could have sworn she was counting them.

"No offense to your uncle," Matt said. "We all do what we can to survive, right?"

He got a flash of comprehension in return. "Survive," she echoed, in that same vibrant, sexy voice. Was that a European accent? Maybe he should post-doc in Eastern Europe.

"If you're right—and I'm not saying you are—why did she tear the place up? And where are her clothes?" Sarah's voice broke through his thoughts.

"Maybe she got here this afternoon while we were in the Exhibit Hall. The taxi driver probably took off right away—he wouldn't want to get stuck behind the tide. Maybe she thought there was a bathroom back here and stripped off to shower? And then when she couldn't find one, she got upset." He looked at the mess and grimaced. "Really upset. Or maybe she's just clumsy."

Sarah frowned. "Stop defending her. This is all still some hare-brained theory." She opened her cell phone. "Joe needs to know about the broken window."

The woman seemed to follow every word. Maybe her English was better than they realized. "What are you working on at home, Miss?" he asked. "Is it something you need a different ecosystem for, or did you just want a peek at life on the other side?"

"The other side?" she echoed.

"A Western marine lab," Matt explained. "To learn how we do

things on this side of the ocean. So you can bring that knowledge back home." He clamped his lips shut to stop babbling.

"Back home," she repeated, peering past Matt and into the tank room. He craned his head to follow her gaze. All the creatures had swum to the front of their aquariums, as if fascinated by the spectacle. Even reclusive Aunt Martha had abandoned his cave to streak along the glass.

Suddenly the girl's gaze sharpened, as if thousands of puzzle pieces inside her head had finally arranged themselves into a coherent whole. "So this is why I am here." She closed her eyes, full lips quivering, as if communing with things unseen.

"She must have a hell of a case of jet lag," Matt whispered to Sarah.

A long pause, as if the woman was waiting for the right translation to rise to the forefront of her mind. "Matt. Sarah. I… apologize."

Sarah hesitated. Matt gave her an imploring look. She sighed, then flipped her phone shut. "Do you have a passport? Papers?" she demanded.

"A suitcase?" Matt added. "Pants? A shirt?"

The girl looked down at herself, then at them, as if registering her nakedness for the first time. She stared at her fingers, wiggling them, then looked up. The panic in her eyes twisted Matt's heart. "When I arrived here, I lost everything."

"Damn airlines." Sarah sighed. "You'll have to file a claim. Matt, can you start digging through this mess to find her clothes?"

"You know what, Sarah? It looks like our visitor's had a pretty rough trip. And anything she owns might be covered with broken glass. Probably not safe to wear.

"Let's lend her some spare clothes—she looks about Jane's size, she always leaves some sweats here—and sweep up this mess, then head out for something to eat. She can crash on my couch until you get her registered and find her a dorm room. We'll get it all figured out after tomorrow's Open House. Okay?"

Sarah's lips pulled into a straight line. "I don't think that's such a good idea."

"I don't think upsetting Joe, or his new foreign friend, is a good idea either. Didn't he say the uncle promised him a chance to work on some disappearing ice? Just think how nice that would be."

"For Joe?"

"For us." Matt lifted a hand to the woman and helped her to her feet. "Let's roll up our sleeves and then we'll grab some dinner. Sushi okay?"

* * *

"Where are we going?" I said, testing my new voice, new limbs, the new words I had enveloped from reading thousands of pages before you discovered me.

You had draped my body with clothes similar to those you yourself wore. I was certain my feet would function more smoothly if I removed the objects you had secured them in, but you shook your head when I started to do so. Unlike you, I learn quickly. The sandals remained. As did the coverings that encased my limbs, and the heavy coat Sarah had draped across my shoulders.

You opened the side of a large shell and eased me inside. My heart leapt. If you travelled in shells as some of us did, perhaps we were more similar than I had thought. Perhaps my mission was not doomed before it began. Perhaps…a new feeling stirred deep within, at once foreign and familiar. Hope.

"Seafood. Sushi." You pulled an object from your pocket. It looked like sea glass, all shiny and smooth, phosphorus darting across its surface.

"Jane and her housemate Hal are joining us. She wants to meet you. Sarah will be there as soon as she's done inserting the new tank labels.

I could've invited Joe, but more is not always merrier." You smiled, and my lips moved in response. And something more—a warmth that started in the middle of my chest and spread through my new body.

You eased the shell onto a road, and tiny rivulets of Wetworld coursed around it as you moved it forward. "You must be ravenous," you said, glancing at me over your shoulder.

You were wrong. I found my new limbs, and the sights, sounds, smells, and perceptions of Dryworld so overwhelming, I could have starved before realizing I needed to eat. But then I noticed something unusual.

"My mouth. It is dry."

"You're probably dehydrated. Have something to drink." You reached out and grabbed a plastic bottle, twisted the top off and handed it to me. It was filled with clear liquid. Hundreds of thousands of those bottles littered Wetworld. Now I knew what they were for. I put it to my lips and sipped, like I had seen someone do in the pictures in one of the many magazines I had perused. The lack of salt made me nearly gag, but I could sense immediately it was what this body craved—not just craved, but depended on to survive.

I tried some new words. "Thank you. That was refreshing."

A line I had not noticed before deepened between your eyes. "Say, what country are you from? Your English is really good."

I shook my head, mimicking your earlier movement. Too quickly, though—dizziness filled me, and I slumped forward.

"Sorry, stranger. Eat first, talk later."

Your shell stopped, and we climbed out. The uneven surface made me stumble. When you took my arm to steady me, a warmth filled me that had nothing to do with your skin brushing against my own. I shivered. What other surprises waited for me in Dryworld?

You stopped beside a dark wall, pushing through an opening to reveal a large cave. For a moment I felt frightened, a strange, disorienting sensation that clouded my judgment, altered my perceptions.

I knew your species was shortsighted, but to enter another creature's cave uninvited was nothing short of lunacy.

Before I could bolt, you slipped your arm around me and gently urged me inside. No grouper rushed to attack, no venomous eel streaked towards us. There were only humans and air and darkness, chairs and tables and flickering lights.

"They're waving to us. It's late. I bet they're starving."

For a sickening moment, I thought you meant to feast on me. Then you took my arm, and my limbs relaxed. I didn't understand it, my love, that instant sense of safety. I still do not, but from the first moment, I trusted you.

We walked towards the others, and I squeezed my limbs into a chair to blend in with the rest of you. Jane—I recognized her face, though all of you looked so different without a sheet of glass distorting your features—handed me a piece of paper and a pencil. She did not smile.

"Matt texted that Joe brought in a new student. I don't know why he thought he needed someone."

"Chill, Jane," you told her. Her lips drew into a pout.

"Is this your first time in a sushi place?" you asked me. "I can order for you, if you want."

"Thank you." I had no idea what you meant. While I struggled to mimic your actions, your speech, I felt as vulnerable as newly hatched spawn.

The human sitting beside Jane spoke to Matt. "Who's your date, man? She's hot." His grin reminded me of a stonefish. "I'm Hal. What's your name?"

It took me a while to realize his question was meant for me. All I could think of was my missing limbs, and how I longed for their familiarity, their strength, to feel complete. "I am Eight."

"Ate? Like, I ate fish for dinner?" Jane laughed.

The others joined her, a low, sloshing sound like the tide coming in. I realized I liked human voices better in chorus. Alone, they felt like an attack. Speaking in chorus diluted the threat.

"Or pieces of eight?" Hal distorted his voice. "Fifteen men on a dead man's chest?"

My human back stiffened. Many more than fifteen men must die. But how could he know that?

"Or 'Eight is Enough'?" I hadn't noticed Sarah slip into the chair on Matt's other side.

"More than enough," Jane muttered.

My face grew hot, as if different fronts warred beneath my flesh. My human limbs tensed for an attack.

You frowned at Jane, and she flushed. Then you lifted a glass of fluid and held it in front of you. "To Eight, the newest addition to our lab. May your time here bring good results."

"What made you pick us?" Jane's voice rose at the end of her sentence, like a fish that had ventured out of its depth and shot too quickly towards the surface.

Before I could reply, a human grasping a container of prey came to our table. The others reached eagerly towards the colorful array. I smelled tuna and eel, salmon and shrimp and crab.

When Wetworld creatures feed, some rend and tear our prey, some envelop, some trap. But these fish had been mutilated, flesh sliced from the bone.

Oblivious to my distress, you set some pieces on a plate and placed it on the table before me. "Dig in. Or there won't be any left."

I grabbed the food and darted away, looking for somewhere private to crouch while I ingested dead prey like a scavenger. I settled beside an empty table, crouching low. My new fingers poked at lumps of tissue. Without its essence to envelop, what would sustain me?

I heard a rustle and looked up. "Eight, this is a modern sushi place, not a traditional Japanese restaurant. We sit on the seats, not on the floor."

I hunched over my plate and turned away, willing you gone.

Instead of backing off, you eased down beside me. "Hey, are you okay?"

"Find your own den," I hissed. You looked hurt, an otter reprimanded by an elder. Obediently you rose and returned to the others. I heard the word "issues."

I breathed in dry air, listened to speech and laughter, my task suddenly overwhelming. Octopi are solitary creatures, but at that moment, I felt something I had never felt before—not in the ocean, not in the glass tank, not even the first time I lifted a tentacle and found a human limb had replaced it.

Like a surge of tide, loneliness coursed through me. My eyes watered, and a burning, stinging trail of saltwater flooded my cheeks.

When the human returned to your table with another tray, you chose more food and carried it over to me. This time I did not protest when you settled beside me. You placed your arm across my shoulders, warm and comforting, like a sheltering kelp forest. So enmeshed was I in these new sensations that it took me a while to notice a new sound, high and whining and shrill, growing louder and louder until I thought my new head would burst.

I scrambled to my feet, food flying. "What is that?"

You rose more slowly, rubbing your knees. "Music too loud for you? I guess we're all used to it. I can ask them to turn it down."

I pointed towards a set of doors at the back of the cave, my hand trembling. "Are there sharks back there? Something is screaming." The sound rose again, then an abrupt silence. I slumped back into the booth, shaking.

"That's the kitchen, where they prepare the food. They make the sushi and sashimi, fry shrimp, boil lobster."

That was what I had heard, a lobster.

"They boil their prey alive! That is beyond barbaric."

You shrugged. "People say it tastes better. I wouldn't know."

"You don't eat them?"

You flashed your teeth. "Not at thirty bucks a pop, on a grad student stipend." You squeezed my shoulders and again I felt no threat, only warmth. "Hey, I have an idea. Why don't we take off and get some ice cream?"

I followed you to where the others were still feeding. You pushed my limbs through the holes in Sarah's coat. It was not a new coat, nor a particularly stylish one—at least, not according to the magazines I had enveloped. The color was a dull brownish green, like dank seaweed. But it kept my Dryworld form warm, and for that I was grateful.

"Where are you going?" Jane's voice was as sharp as coral.

"I'm taking Eight for some ice cream. I don't think sushi's her thing." You threw some green paper on the table. "Later, guys."

"Are you going out after? Maybe we can meet you." Jane again, gaze fixed on you. Beside her Hal squirmed in his seat, not unlike an octopus.

You frowned. "I thought you had a study group tonight."

Jane's gaze did not leave your face. "I blew it off to have dinner with you. No biggie." Her full lips pursed. "I hardly ever get to see you outside of the lab anymore."

You took a step back. "I'm flattered, but with the Open House tomorrow, I'm opting for an early night. See you guys tomorrow."

Jane's lips folded into a pout. I had read about those as well. "Just one drink?"

"Maybe tomorrow night, okay?" Your arm tightened across my shoulders. "Eight's had a day. She needs a shower and some sleep."

"Where is she staying?" Jane's cheek muscles tensed, a barracuda poised to lunge.

"At my place, until Sarah finds her a dorm room."

"Oh." Layers of meaning in that one word.

Your eyes narrowed. "Unless you want to volunteer your couch?"

Jane's eyes met mine. They were as blue as a white shark's, and as cold. I stared back until she looked away.

"I don't think so." Jane's tone matched the chill in her gaze. "She's all yours."

* * *

"So what are we going to feed you?" You draped a new moist cloth against my forehead. "Think you're done yet?"

I shook my head, knees pressed against the smooth cold floor, hands gripping the sides of the "throne." My stomach roiled, and once again its contents landed in the water at the bottom of the bowl. You pulled the silver handle, and a whirlpool sucked the spoiled food away. Fascinating.

"I am so sorry." Your forehead puckered. "Maybe you're lactose intolerant? Joe said somewhere in Eastern Europe, right? You must be, with that olive skin and black hair. I should have known better."

My stomach lurched again, even though it was empty. "I need to get used to your feed."

"Food." You wet another cloth, with warm water this time, and ran it across my lips. I caught it between my teeth, sucking out the liquid.

"Don't do that. If you're thirsty, I'll make you some tea."

"Tea?"

"Chamomile. I think Jane left some." You guided me to your couch, then ducked into a smaller cave, where you started banging the walls open and shut. "Found it."

"Jane was in your cave—here?" That thought made my new back stiffen.

"We had a thing for a few weeks." More banging, and the sound of running water. "It was a mistake."

I had read that word, but not in this context. "You mean, like wearing knee socks with sandals?"

You chuckled as you set a cup of steaming water on the low table. Despite my discomfort, I basked in the sound. You stroked the top of my head, and my human scalp tingled in response.

"Feeling any better?" You sat beside me and patted my shoulder.

My stomach had finally calmed. I clasped your hand and drew it along the side of my face, reveling in the sensation of your fingers against my skin. In my mind's eye I saw Aunt Martha streaking back and forth in her aquarium, signaling a warning. *Too soon.*

But I did not let go. As you reached up to stroke my hair, I thought, *humans are not the only ones who make mistakes.*

* * *

The next morning, when rays of sun pushed through the glass walls—windows—into the living room, I bolted upright. This sensation, tumbling into an oblivion akin to death, is not what we do in Wetworld, where danger lurks around every crevasse, prey washes forward with every new front. We sleep with one eye open—both eyes, actually. Our rest occurs deep within us. We are rarely exhausted. To ignore the need for rest makes one weak. Weakness brings death.

The toilet flushed. A moment later you walked into the living room and knelt beside me. "How're you doing this morning?"

"Better. Matt." My lips curved upwards as I savored the feeling of your name in my mouth. You mimicked me, and I realized I was smiling. Another new sensation. Happy, sad, angry, thoughtful—so many shades of being, shifting constantly, like sunlight filtered through rolling waves. I felt disoriented, almost giddy, and then something so foreign I had to search for the corresponding word. Sympathy. For if your emotions consistently overrode logic, like silt clouding churning waters, was it any wonder your species made the choices you did?

"Are you ready for the Open House?" you said.

For an absurd moment, I thought you meant to place me back inside my tank. I recoiled, limbs closing protectively around my vital organs.

"Hey, no worries. I'll just tell Joe you weren't feeling well."

"Joe."

"Yeah, Joe. The asshole head of the lab? The guy responsible for your transfer?"

I sucked in my breath so deeply I thought my stomach and backbone would collide. "Joe is the reason I transformed?"

You laughed, a charming sound like dolphins frolicking through waves. They are more at risk than my kind, those large, lively, mammals, and not nearly as intelligent, but sometimes, watching their endless joy, I grow wistful.

"Not transformed. Transferred. Joe gave you a spot in his lab in exchange for something your uncle did for him. So if you're up for it, I'd put in an appearance, show you're motivated, you know? You don't have to do much, Sarah has it covered. But if you think you're going to hurl again, stay here. I'll tell Joe you've got jet lag." You glanced at your phone. "We need to move faster, though, if you're coming."

I refused your offer of breakfast, although I could feel weakness creeping inside me, and knew I must find nourishment soon. Why did accompanying you seem more important than feeding myself? I pushed that uncomfortable thought to the back of my new mind—easy to do, human minds being so distractible—and watched you cover your feet.

"Why do you do that? Does it not impair your balance, your ability to hunt, and to pivot from danger?"

Your lip quirked, and I felt a tingle of triumph. Smiles, grins...I was beginning to appreciate Dryworld's subtle shifts in communication. Useful, but even more than that, oddly stimulating, as you might feel when you discovered why a dog wags its tail, or a cat rubs up against your legs. Endearing.

"I've often wondered. But, you know," you handed me the sandals I wore yesterday. "Shirts and shoes required."

We rode in your giant shell—car—to the lab. I had been too weary, too confused to appreciate this new mode of movement the night before. Straight lines, right-angled turns, each of you so rigidly in place as you wove around one another.

On your land, you breached no boundaries. But when you entered mine, you ignored them as if they did not exist. It should have told me something, but I was still as blind as an anemone.

You pulled into a clearing and stopped the car. "Hope you don't mind a bit of a walk? The shuttles won't start till half an hour before we open to the public, and it's just not safe to park cars at the lab these days. The tides are too unpredictable."

I fell into step beside you. In the distance, Wetworld encroached. Silver ribbons streamed past the sandy beaches, broke around tree trunks, splashed across roads. Not yet.

Oblivious, you waved a hand at the cluster of buildings. "The smaller ones are the individual labs, and this big setup right next to our office is the Exhibit Hall. We also have a whale skeleton and a few outdoor telescopes, but today's focus is the Hall, and our lab."

We walked up the steps. How ironic, to see your cave from the outside.

"Let's check on the specimens first," you said. "Then I'll show you the Hall."

We walked through your office and into the tank room, as you called it. When we entered the darkness, my fellow creatures approached the front of their prisons. My human mouth went dry. Why did I suddenly feel like a traitor?

The wolf eel you called Aunt Martha flowed from his cave. Our eyes met. Before we could communicate you tapped lightly on the glass, and he backed away.

You frowned. "They're still kind of off. I can't figure out why. Sarah thinks we're overfeeding, but we haven't changed anything." You adjusted covers, checked thermometers, straightened information sheets. So much attention, my love, yet their essences eluded you.

"I wish they'd perk up." You frowned. "People like to see the fish doing something, you know? They get bored when they're just sitting there."

My stomach sank as I realized that you didn't, couldn't understand. "What else can they do but sit there? In these cramped, sterile prisons?"

Your lips pulled into a frown. I felt as if I had swum too close to coral and scraped myself.

"Look, Eight, don't go all granola on Joe, okay? Or he'll ship you back to your uncle before you can say 'seaweed', grant or no grant."

We left the room, the fish gazing after me.

"Let me show you the Exhibit Hall, where you'll be helping out." We crossed the courtyard to the adjacent building, a huge, deep cavern. Fascinated, I gazed into its vastness.

Colorful images of ocean life lined the walls, and large models of Wetworld life peppered the interior.

Above our heads, a school of sharks threw grim shadows all around us. I grabbed your arm, meaning to pull you to safety, until I realized they were frozen in space.

"Those sharks…" I gestured upwards. "Why are they not moving? Most will die if they keep still."

"Yeah, well, our budget is the size of a pond, not an ocean. We got them used from an aquarium that upgraded. Mechanical sharks will have to wait."

We strolled through the exhibits, and you explained the purpose of each one. A deep sadness filled me. How could you know so much, yet understand so little?

In the middle of the hall sat a large television set, benches grouped in front of it. On the screen, a woman stood before a snow-covered mountain, talking about the threat of climate change. Calving icebergs plunged into the sea, sending up massive plumes of icy spray.

The picture changed to a starving polar bear roaming land that was never meant to see the sun, then flashed to frantic salmon battling their way through too-warm waters. The woman appeared again, alongside a chart of rising ocean waters. Her tone was grim, her expression stern.

So it had begun.

Your hands knotted as we watched the screen. "It's kind of scary, you know? No one's sure why it's happening so fast, all of a sudden. Even over the last few months, the warming rate is increasing exponentially. They think it's coming from below, not above. And these tides the last few weeks—none of it makes sense." Your worried gaze met mine. "If this keeps up, I'm not sure we can stop it."

I almost told you everything. Right there, underneath the false sharks, beside the empty benches.

Remember your purpose. The wolf eel's thoughts pulsed through my mind.

I stumbled and clutched your arm.

"Eight, are you really okay? Maybe you should have stayed home."

For an absurd moment, I thought you were speaking of Wetworld.

I pushed past you, toward the giant replicas of clamshells crouched on a square of carpeted floor. My voice shook as I changed the subject.

"Clams are much, much smaller than that."

"Yeah, this is for the kids to play on, so they don't wreck the rest of the room. Sarah's idea, she has two rambunctious nephews. You'll meet them later."

But I was streaking towards an alcove we had not yet explored, where a cluster of tables bunched in a half-circle. Each receptacle held a few inches of brackish water, crowded with sea life frantically seeking shelter beneath skimpy ropes of kelp. A sign above said, "Tide Pools."

"Where are the rocks?" I said. "There's not enough kelp to cover these creatures. It is their nature to hide."

You shook your head—a new variation on the frown. "If we cover them, people can't see them."

"But they don't want to be seen!"

Something brushed my shoulder. I whirled, ready to strike, but it was only a human.

"Joe." Your smile became rigid as you gestured around the room. "Sarah's done a brilliant job, hasn't she?"

Joe did not return your smile. "How did that storeroom window get broken?"

Your gaze slanted to me, then returned to the floor. You shoved your hand in your pockets. "It was a mistake. Luckily it faces the back courtyard, so none of the visitors can see it. I'll get it fixed tomorrow."

"How does a window get broken by mistake?" Joe's voice hissed like an underwater geyser, spraying heat and unpleasantness.

"This is the mistake." I did not realize I had spoken until I heard my own voice. "These creatures need more protection, or they will die of fright."

"Shock, she means." You put your hand on my arm. "This is Eight, your friend's niece. She arrived yesterday just after you left."

Joe's gaze, as unwavering as a shark's, locked onto mine. "Eight? What kind of a name is that?"

Quickly you came to my rescue. "It's the closest we can pronounce it, sir."

"Are you studying the results of shock on marine life?" Joe said. "I need an extra pair of hands at the dissection demonstration later. You can chart the results."

Joe's cell phone chimed. He looked at the screen and put it to his ear. As he walked away, he called back over his shoulder, "Eleven o'clock, Ettie. Be on time."

I looked at you, my eyes blank. "The…what?"

Your eyebrows rose. "The dissection room. Where we cut fish open to see what's inside."

"Like the prey you ate in the cave last night? Joe slices them apart?" I clutched your arm, amazed at how natural the gesture felt. Almost as if I had claimed a new tentacle. Startled, I dropped it and stepped back, bumping hard against something. I, the most graceful of Wet-world denizens, who streams through our viscous atmosphere like a jet of phosphorous, stumbled and sprawled on the ground like a sea slug. Vulnerable. Exposed.

Instinct took over. Wave after wave of ink pulsed through my human body, pooling on the floor around me. In my present form, it showed as scarlet, not black. No camouflage, this; your shocked expression told me that I had drawn unwanted attention.

"Holy shit, Eight! Are you all right?" You whirled to confront Jane, who was rubbing her elbow. "What the hell did you do to her?"

"Whoa, mister. She bumped me." The hurt in her tone was palpable.

Sarah appeared and thrust a thick wad of paper towels at me. "Hold those against the wound. So much blood!"

You pulled your phone from your shirt pocket. "I'm calling an ambulance."

"No! I am not hurt." I pressed the towels between my legs and scrambled to my feet. Crimson ink dripped down my legs, staining my clothes. "I didn't expect to release…" I clamped my lips shut, horrified at how quickly this human tongue had nearly betrayed me.

Sarah's expression shifted from worried to sympathetic. I wondered again how humans, whom we consider slower than sea snails, managed instantaneous shifts in perception.

"The flight probably messed up your cycle," she told me. "Air travel can do that, especially when you go through a gazillion time changes.

"Put your phone away, Matt. Eight's embarrassed enough as it is. You and Jane mop up while I take her to the shower and find her some new duds. And some supplies."

"But…what happened?" You looked as bewildered as a fish that had strayed from its school.

Jane peeled more paper towels apart and started dabbing at the mess. "Get a clue, Matt. And the mop."

* * *

Sarah showed me the shower, and I savored the warm spray until it turned icy. Then I dried myself on a rough piece of fabric—a concept I could not quite take in, to dry myself—and dressed, being careful to line the inside pants with the thick wad of not-quite paper. Now that I had released, it would normally take some time to build up my reserves. But in this new body I could take no chances.

"Feel better?" Sarah asked.

I nodded.

"Good. Ready to work?" Her expression changed again, this time apologetic. "If we weren't so short-staffed, I'd tell you to sit down and relax. But three of my volunteers couldn't get through flooded roads. Cramps?"

Again, Sarah switched from one topic to another with no warning. "No. Thank you." I stopped talking when I realized cramps were not something she was offering me. I made a note to research cramps and time zones as I followed Sarah back through the outer buildings to the exhibit hall, sidestepping puddles. "Joe asked me to help at the dissection table. At eleven o'clock."

"It's ten-forty." Her gaze studied my face. "You still look a little pale. Tell you what. You fill in for me at the hands-on, and I'll cover for you with Joe. You can help him cut up fish this afternoon."

She pointed towards the tide pool exhibit. "Go share that table with Jane."

Jane took a grudging step sideways as I approached, like a bad-tempered crab.

"Where's Sarah? We were supposed to be partners."

"Joe needed her."

"Have you ever manned an exhibit before?"

I shook my head.

"Perfect," Jane muttered. "I used to volunteer at Sea World. The kids want to touch things. Make sure they don't get too rough." She gestured beneath the table. "If you think a specimen is getting too much love, drop it in the bucket here and put out something new.

"The adults ask the questions. Kids just want to play. Which is fine, but don't lose sight of what the kids are doing while you talk to their parents."

I pushed my hand through the water. It blurred, reforming as a tentacle. I snatched it back, and it instantly transformed into a hand.

Had that really happened? I wriggled my fingers, wondering if Jane had glimpsed it, too. But she was busy filling cans with colored sticks.

An alarm filled the air, sound pulsing from every corner of the room. My body tensed. In my mind's eye I could see ocean waters pour through the hall, froth around the benches, hear screams and the crack of floating items crashing against the walls. I looked around wildly, needing to see you, to make sure you were safe.

Nothing had changed.

"Showtime," Jane muttered. "Don't look so panicked, Eight. They're just kids."

Someone flung the doors open, and the room flooded with humans. The noise level rose until I thought the walls would collapse from the vibrations. Smaller humans—children—rushed towards us, some alone, some tugging at adults. They swarmed the shallow tanks like frenzied sharks, hands churning the water. "Are they always so oblivious to their surroundings? If these children were fish, they would all have been eaten by now," I said to Jane.

Her lip twitched. "Very funny, Eight."

I saw rather than heard Jane scolding them, but the children ignored her instructions, their chatter high and shrill as dolphins.

"Stop!" My voice reverberated through the hall like a whale call, high and insistent. Perhaps not all of me had been left behind.

The children quieted. I pointed to the tide pool before me. "These creatures live in a quiet world, where sounds are muted by water, broken by rocks, softened by sand." The lines from the marine books I had enveloped rolled from my tongue like a wave.

A child reached into the pool, and I hissed. She looked up, gaze as soft as a baby seal. "But my mom said we could play with them."

"Learn about them." Unexpectedly, Jane came to my rescue. "They're not stuffed animals, or kittens. How would you feel if a giant hand reached into your room and grabbed you?"

She used the silence to pick up a sea star. I winced as the creature stiffened its limbs, fighting for survival.

A girl tugged at her mom's hand, then pointed at me. "Mom, look!"

I felt a tug at my scalp. My human hair was springing up in all directions, weaving through the air as if it was water.

"She just arrived here," Jane hastily told the children, while I did my best to twist the strands into submission. "Hair can do funny things in a new climate." She held out the sea star. "Touch it gently. Everyone gets one pat, then it needs to go back in the tank to breathe."

A boy's arm plunged through the water and emerged with a wriggling sea cucumber. "Look what I got!"

I pried it from his chubby fists and placed it carefully in the water. It sank behind a bit of kelp, sides pulsing. "It is not meant to be handled. Not unless you plan to eat it."

"But this is the touch tank!" Evading me, his hand plunged into the water. The creature eviscerated, leaving a jet of slime. "Gross!"

"Leave it alone!" I snapped.

Jane gave me a sharp look, and I modulated my tone. "That's how it protects itself from predators." I pointed across the hall to the movie screen, which was still playing to empty benches. Another iceberg broke and fell, its massive splash filling the screen. "Why don't you go over there and learn about the ocean?"

He shook his head, lower lip thrust forward like a grouper. "I want a turn with that."

I glanced back to the table, where a girl tugged at the spiny legs of a brittle star. Jane, busy preventing another group of children from shredding the tentacles of an anemone, did not notice.

Even through the foreign medium of air, I could feel the terror coursing through it. To be stalked, captured, enveloped is our destiny, and the denizens of Wetworld live at peace with the procession of our lives. But whether we are torn to pieces by sharks, stunned by eels, or gulped by tuna, there is a dignity to our passing. A purpose. Just as when two fronts meet, and the weaker gives way to the stronger, prey becomes one with its predator. Each envelopment becomes part of a new beginning.

But to terrify a creature for amusement, entertainment—without conscious thought, my arm shot forward. Suckers popped out along the underside as I slapped the creature from the child's grasp. The sea star tumbled back into the tank while the girl wrung small hands together, shrieking. "Mom! Mom! It stung me…it stung me!"

My arm snapped back to human form and hung slack, as if aware it had erred. Jane knelt beside the child. Her thumb had swollen to twice its normal size, the flesh puckered and oozing blood. The mother's mouth trembled as she hugged her squalling offspring.

"Let's not panic. I'll find something that can calm an allergic reaction." Jane unhooked a pack from around her waist and split it apart.

From the safety of her mother's arms, the child continued to howl.

I tugged at Jane's arm as she started rummaging through the contents. "Why is she calling attention to herself?"

Jane's eyes narrowed. "What the hell else should she do, Eight? Suck it up like a big girl? She's scared and in pain."

"But she is injured," I explained. "Why is she not hiding her wound? It makes her vulnerable."

"To what? Ridicule? Look around. I don't see anyone laughing." Jane focused on the pack. "Where the hell is the Benadryl?" She glanced up at me. "Eight, can you flag down another docent? Maybe they have something. And an antiseptic cream if you can find one."

I blinked, still not comprehending. "In my world, an injured creature would have been devoured by now."

Jane's mouth dropped open. "I don't know what psychopaths brought you up, but here in the US, we care for our young—especially if they're injured. Now try to find something to help while I get hold of Sarah." Jane pulled a phone from her pocket.

You are the mimic. Help the child. The wolf eel again, though hard to hear his thoughts through the cacophony.

I grabbed a net from the bucket beneath the tank and drew it through the water until I found what I needed. Plucking the creature from the mesh, I rubbed its glistening flesh across the child's wound.

Within seconds, the swelling subsided. The crowd watched wide-eyed as the thumb returned to normal size, the punctures all but disappearing.

"What on earth?" Jane spluttered.

"Sea slugs. They produce a—" even the marine books didn't have the words, since humans had yet to discover why all marine creatures avoided that particular species.

Jane's eyes widened. "Is that what you're researching?"

Before I could reply, the child wailed again. "I can't feel my hand!"

"The numbness wears off quickly." I hoped I was correct.

"No more tide pools today, okay?" Jane patted the child on the shoulder, and then turned to her mother. "None of these creatures are poisonous. I've never seen a reaction like that. Is she allergic to shellfish? Maybe she brushed against one of the mollusks."

The mother shook her head, bewildered. "She eats shrimp by the bucketful."

Jane handed her a tube of ointment. "Just to be safe, I'd rub this on a few times during the day. I am so sorry."

As the pair walked away, Jane faced me, furious. "I saw you slap that sea star out of her hand. Are you crazy?"

I gestured at the tide pool tables. Children were peering at the creatures, but no one else had been brave enough to stick a hand inside. "This is crazy. And wrong."

"What are you talking about? What we do here is important! We're teaching future generations to respect ocean life."

"By disrespecting its inhabitants? Showing them off as if they were replicas, like those false sharks swimming from the ceiling? Suffocating them?"

"We don't suffocate them, Eight! We hold them up for a minute, so the kids can experience them. Big deal."

I wondered if the actual humans found her as annoying as I did. "Would you find it a big deal, if it was happening to you?" My arm shot out and grasped Jane just beneath her chin. As if flicking an errant piece of seaweed from my lair, I shoved her head into the tank.

I meant to submerge her for but an instant. I wanted—needed—her to feel what a Wetworld creature would feel in the same predicament. Rage. Panic. Terror.

But, as I mentioned before, our limbs have minds of their own. Even as I tried to withdraw my arm, my fingers lengthened, wove around her neck and held her down.

Jane clawed at my hand, her gaze frightened and furious. I fought to let her up, but my wayward limb had sucked all my strength into itself, and remained rigid as a coral reef. The harder I tried to free her, the more tenacious my grip became.

Jane's eyes fluttered closed, her struggles grew feeble.

I was afraid to plunge my other arm in the water to try to release my grip, terrified that it, too, would mutiny. My breath grew rapid and shallow. I tried to scream, but no sound emerged from my throat. Desperately I pushed against the table, rocking it back and forth, but the sturdy frame resisted my efforts. I pushed harder, crashing my body into the side over and over, heedless of the pain.

Jane's hand fell from my arm as her life force ebbed away. I clutched the side of the table, yanking with all my strength. One of my legs caught the table leg, and it wobbled. With all the force in my human form, I kicked at the supports. The touch tank crashed to the floor, taking Jane and me with it. Water poured out, carrying the creatures away.

Beneath a layer of kelp, Jane sprawled across the side of the tank, not moving. The color had drained from her face, leaving it fish-belly white. Tangled in strands of kelp, my tentacle fell away from her neck.

I forced it around her chest and squeezed. Nothing. Before exposure to the air could turn it human again, I squeezed again, harder.

An arc of water shot from Jane's mouth. She rolled over and sat upright, gagging and spluttering, wet hair clumped about her face like sea grass. Garish colors streaked her cheeks, making her resemble one of the more flamboyant nudibranchs.

I lay beside her, shivering, bewildered, sounds raining down. Beneath strings of kelp, my tentacle flopped by my side like a beached fish. I heard shouting, and footsteps, and I knew discovery was seconds away.

"Jane! Eight! What happened?"

You knelt beside us. I memorized your face. Once you saw what I was, I knew I would never see that expression again.

But your face did not change. I glanced at my tentacle. Somehow my errant limb had transformed to human shape once more.

"You bitch!" Jane's voice came out in a squeak only you and I could hear. "Matt, she tried to kill me!"

"Jane—"

"She held my face underwater. I couldn't breathe!"

"Is that true, Eight?"

You must have taken my silence for consent. The expression in your eyes made me want to retreat into a cave and never emerge.

"What the hell were you thinking!" you snapped.

I struggled to make you understand—or what was the point of my being here?

"She needs to know how those Wetworld creatures felt when she did the same to them. So she could realize why it is wrong to treat us—them—this way." I reached for your hand, but you pulled away, revulsion etched in every line of your features.

"I realize plenty!" Jane glared at me, teeth chattering. "Do you realize that what you did to me is going to get you sent to jail—maybe even deported?"

You put your arm around Jane. When you spoke, your voice was colder than a winter sea. "How can you be so softhearted about a crab, Eight, and not care anything about Jane? How do you think she felt?"

Jane wept against your chest. A crowd gathered around us. "One of our volunteers slipped, and knocked the tank over," you said. The explanation traveled through the crowd, and parents steered their children clear of us as docents approached with nets, mops and buckets.

"Can you walk?" you asked Jane. She nodded. You helped her to her feet.

"Go dry off and change. Hang out in the office for a bit." You lowered your voice. "I've got some brandy in the bottom drawer of my desk, behind the first-aid kit. It's in a bottle labeled 'rubbing alcohol'. I'll come check on you soon."

"I'll do that. Right after I call the police."

"Give it a minute, okay?" you said. "Let me talk to Eight first."

"Like she talked to me?" Jane limped away, leaving a trail of droplets.

"Where do you think you're going?" you asked as I struggled to my feet, wincing. Air was less forgiving than water.

"Those creatures will die on Dryworld. Someone needs to put them back."

"The docents are taking care of it." You steered me to a small alcove against the wall, tucked away from the main expanse. We sat on a bench. "You're a real piece of work, you know that? That kind of horseplay might go down where you're from, but it's not acceptable here."

"I didn't mean to hurt Jane! Just wet her face for a moment. I was trying to pull her up, not hold her down. But it got stuck." Saltwater sprang from my eyes and dripped down my cheeks. "I pulled as hard as I could, but I couldn't pry it loose. So I knocked over the tank to free her."

"*She* got stuck, Eight. Not *it*. Her hair must have snagged on something." You rummaged in your shirt and brought up a square of fabric. "It's a handkerchief," you said, in response to my puzzled look. "Wipe your eyes and blow your nose. I'm going to try to calm Jane down. Explain that you were trying to save her, not kill her. Maybe I can change her mind about calling the police. But you have to promise me you'll never pull a stunt like that again. Not with her, not with anyone else. No matter how angry you get. Didn't your parents teach you to use your words?"

My parents probably tried to eat me.

"I am an orphan." A word I dredged from Sarah's books.

Your expression softened. "Look, I get that things are different where you come from. I've toured your labs, and you guys are a lot more dramatic, you know? But in the States, we don't push people into fish tanks to prove a point. We talk."

"Like Jane talked to the sea star?"

Your eyebrows drew together. "Eight, we're the humans here, remember? Our safety takes precedence."

For now.

Your gaze held mine, searching for something it could never find. Finally, you reached out and squeezed my shoulder. "Relax, okay? I'll talk to Jane. Maybe we can still salvage this."

I took a deep breath of air, then another, fighting for calm. The floor had been mopped, the tank righted and refilled. Children crowded round, touching, squeezing, as if nothing had happened. Like the ocean, ever changing, ever timeless.

"I know Jane is upset," I said. "But we—they—deserve better. Before there's no turning back." You looked skeptical, and I persisted. "How can you be so certain that you—we—decide the world's fate? How can you prepare for an enemy you cannot comprehend? One that you don't even acknowledge?" I clamped my lips shut, terrified at what I had almost revealed.

But I need not have worried. Once again, you failed to understand. You leaned closer. I resisted the urge to lift my hand to your face, to trace the creases in your skin. Looking at you made me long for something I could not comprehend.

"Are you talking about climate change? That's what this is all about, Eight. These creatures are ambassadors. When a kid touches one, it makes it real. Down the line, when it comes time to vote on establishing a marine preserve, or funding an aquarium, or not tossing trash into the ocean—that touch might make all the difference."

"It is too late." I hadn't realized I had spoken until my words filled the air.

"What's too late?"

"For your young to respect Wetworld."

You squeezed my hand, and warmth flooded me. "Don't be a defeatist, Eight. It's never too late."

I followed you out of the Exhibit Hall. The gravel walkways glistened in the pale sunlight. You kicked at a string of seaweed. "What the heck? The tides never come up this far."

Not yet. My task is not complete. I sent my thoughts towards Wetworld, but no glimmer of consciousness answered.

We trudged up the steps to the office and into the tank room, the darkness a stark contrast to the morning sunshine.

"We don't open this room to the public for another hour, so it's nice and quiet. Just hang out until your clothes dry."

I shivered, and you took off your sweater and draped it around me. The fishes swam forward, their curiosity almost palpable. We stopped in front of the empty octopus tank. You looked at me, then at the water, and sighed. "Funny, isn't it? My project vanishes, you show up…"

I sucked in my breath, cold air clinging to each tooth. But you are human, my love. The obvious eludes you.

"Your project?"

"I study mollusks. The octopus was a lucky find, you know? They're so solitary, so good at blending in—and smart! No one understands what they're capable of." Your tone grew wistful. "Sarah thinks I'm pathetic, but I really felt a connection."

The next words out of my mouth surprised me. "They are not solitary. They have their limbs."

"Their tentacles are company?"

"Like houseguests. Except they never depart."

You reached in and stirred the water with your finger, leaving small ripples. The sight of them stirred something within me, something deep and primal.

"This one departed. We've looked everywhere."

Not everywhere.

"I'm afraid she slipped into Aunt Martha's tank and died. Maybe the pH was too different, or Martha got tired of visitors." Your shoulders slumped. "I miss her."

"Wolf eels don't hurt octopi. Cave dwellers stick together."

Your expression brightened, like surf lit by the sun.

I touched the glass. The wolf eel thrust his nose to meet it, as if an invisible wall did not separate us. Even while I remained in human form, his consciousness pulsed through me.

The tides are rising.

I need more time.

The eel backed away, his movements sluggish.

I frowned. "He looks ill."

You nodded. "Aunt Martha's getting old. Sarah rescued him right after I came here as an undergrad, nine years ago. Some kids were torturing him, poking him with sticks." You tapped the glass, and the eel vanished into its cave.

"Why do you call him 'Aunt' Martha, when he's male?"

"Sarah said he reminded her of her great-aunt. Feisty, not taking crap from anyone." Your head tilted to one side. "Hey, how did you know he's a 'he'?"

I reminded myself to be more careful. I had always thought you the blind ones, like the creatures from our depths who find illumination unbearable. Yet I caught myself experiencing the eel through new eyes, with new senses. Not as a fellow creature, but as a specimen.

"His atmosphere does not suit him. He needs real seawater." *As do I.* Without thinking, I lowered my hand into the water.

"Eight! Be careful!" Before my fingers could blur and reshape, you jerked my hand from the tank. "He could bite you!"

Footsteps sounded from behind us. "Serve her right." Jane's hoarse voice cut through the darkness.

You turned and pulled Jane close. "How are you doing, honey?"

She shrugged your arm away. Even in the dimness, I could see dark circles staining her neck. "I grabbed that same sea slug and ran it over my skin. Just like that," Jane snapped two fingers together, "the swelling went down." Her eyes narrowed. "How did you *know*?"

"Jane, I am sorry. I mean, I am glad your neck is better. I am sorry for what I did."

"Eight was trying to pull you up," you told her. "Not hold you down. She said your hair snagged on something. That's why she upset the table. To save you. Can you forgive her?"

Jane's damp curls flew from side to side. "I almost *drowned*."

You reached out and stroked her cheek. My body stiffened. "Look, I know it was scary. Eight swears never to do anything like that again. Can't we let it rest?"

Jane swelled like a puffer fish. She knocked your hand away. "Let it rest? Let it rest?"

"No rest for the weary, kids." Sarah's voice cut through the gloom. "I need all of you back on the floor, now."

Before Jane could respond, Sarah glanced at her wrist and looked up at me. "Better hurry, Eight. You're next up at dissection."

"She's never been to Joe's lab," you said quickly. "I'll take her."

Sarah shook her head. "You two both have school groups waiting. That is, if you're up for it, Jane? I heard a table collapsed on you. I'm so sorry, I thought they were sturdier. Are you up for leading a tour?"

"I could do that," I said. "Lead a school group."

Jane snorted. "Yeah, we've seen how great you are with kids." She lifted her hair, and Sarah gasped at the bruises circling her neck. "Did you see what she did to me?"

"It was an accident," you broke in. "Eight didn't mean it."

"The hell she didn't!"

Sarah turned towards me, shock written across her face. "Eight? Did you do that to Jane?"

In Wetworld, we evade predators by flight or camouflage. Your way is different, my love, though no less effective. "What I did is not important," I answered. "What Jane did will earn her a place at any marine program in Dryworld—I mean, your world."

Jane gazed at me for a long moment. "The sea slug?" she said softly. "But you already knew what it could do."

"Only in theory," I said. "The real discovery is yours, if..." I let my voice trail off.

"I'll think about it," Jane said finally.

Sarah's cell phone chirped, and she studied the screen before jamming it back into her pocket.

"We don't have time to think. Jane, Matt—school groups. Eight, you're with Joe. Move!" She raced from the room.

Jane tugged your arm. "Let's go, Matt. The only thing worse than leading a group of kids is leading a group of antsy kids who've been standing around too long." She looked over her shoulder at me as she turned away. "This isn't finished."

"I'll catch up." Ignoring Jane's glare, you walked me outside and pointed towards a cluster of buildings. Behind them, the sea pounded and foamed.

"See that green flag? Joe's lab is over there."

"What do I do?"

"Whatever he says. No matter how much of a jerk he is, just don't piss him off, okay? He's still the man." You squeezed my arm, then loped away.

I started towards the building, still marveling at how two limbs propelled the rest. In Wetworld, I would have had a mutiny if my other appendages ceased their work.

I pushed open the door beneath the flag.

A gruff voice addressed me. "Where do you think you're going?"

I whirled to face this new threat. A man in khaki clothing, 'Security' written above his heart, stared at me with narrowed eyes. I straightened my legs and lowered my arms.

"I am here to assist Joe. Sarah sent me."

"Where's your badge, miss?"

"I have no badge. I am the transformed—transfer student. I arrived last night."

"Shoulda given you a badge." He scrawled something on a piece of paper and handed it to me. "Stick this on your shirt. It'll have to do."

I pressed the paper against my shirt. As soon as I took my hand away, it fluttered to the floor.

The guard clambered from his seat and picked up the paper, then tore it in two. His hand pressed half of it just below my collarbone. "Foreigners." A world of scorn in that one word.

If you only knew.

I hurried down the hall. The door to Joe's lab was propped open, and I slipped inside. It smelled of marine life and terror. Above us, harsh lights illuminated the stark space. I felt as if I had plummeted to the depths, where only the eerie glow of phosphorous fishes pierce the gloom.

Students milled around a gleaming silver table, asking Joe questions. He looked up and gestured me to his side.

"This is Etty, our new exchange student." Joe pulled a fish out of a bucket near his feet and tossed it on the table. It flopped, startled. "This should be right up your alley."

My jaw dropped.

"Etty here's studying the effect of stress on marine life." Joe gestured to the wriggling fish. "It doesn't get more stressful than this."

A nervous titter ran through the group, a current of unease even I could feel. It made me soften towards them. And yet, why did they participate in this monstrous act of cruelty?

The fish thrashed and gasped, its life force ebbing away. Quickly I grabbed it and tossed it back into the bucket. I didn't realize I'd been holding my breath until I saw the fish right itself and swim around, butting its head against the sides, frantic for escape.

Joe's eyebrows drew together, a wave about to break. "Why'd you do that, Etty? The students were timing it, to see how long it could last out of the water before we dissect it." His shark eyes bored into me. "Grab another one. We'll have to start the experiment over." He turned to the students. "If you go into marine biology, you need lots of patience. It's not like physics, or chemistry, where you control the substance you're working with. These are living creatures, and therefore, unpredictable." He winked. "Like lab assistants."

How stressful would it be for you, Joe, if I pulled you into a crevasse and timed your demise?

My human arms tingled, the digits at the ends of them rigid. But I had promised you I would use my words. I kept my hands at my sides as I addressed the class, although I could feel my hair twist and writhe around my frame, a visual counterpart to my inner distress.

The students stared, and I willed my hair to stillness. "Ocean creatures kill to feed. They do not torture their prey—they envelop it." I pointed to the dissection table, gleaming coldly beneath the flickering lights, the stained scalpel, the thin film of blood coating the surface. "This experiment is inhumane. You are better than this."

An uneasy murmur filled the room, like a drone of sand fleas.

Joe glared at me. "Etty, I know this seems harsh. We're not heartless, though. We don't make creatures suffer for the fun of it. But do you know how many cures have come out of the ocean? Shark cartilage, healing jells from seaweed—much of what we use to fight cancer comes from seawater.

"Everything we do here is for the good of humanity. Wouldn't you rather have a shark suffer than, say, your little brother?"

"A shark is my little brother," I muttered, but Joe had already plucked a new victim from the bucket. As if sensing the changing mood of his audience, the knife sliced quickly, a jaw snapping. The fish lurched and then lay still, blood pooling on the table. There were whispers of "ew" and "gross" as the students pressed forward.

Joe offered me the scalpel. "Care to do the honors?"

I took a step back, having no idea what he wanted from me. Joe's expression darkened. "They're not puppies, Etty, they're fish. If you have a problem with this, why did you go into marine biology in the first place?"

"It was the only course open to me."

"Well, if you want a recommendation, I suggest you change your tune." At my blank look, Joe explained, "It means, adjust your attitude."

Another titter, this time louder. Like a shift in a school of fish, the emotions in the room shifted to Joe's point of view.

"Marine scientists study marine life. That's our purpose. If you don't like it..." Joe shrugged thick shoulders.

I struggled to put my thoughts into words, marveling at the restraint it entailed, wishing you had harnessed that restraint when making decisions about your surroundings. "You study marine death, not marine life. Most ocean creatures have short lives. To rob them of their brief time, for your own curiosity—we—I—cannot countenance it. Creatures prey on others to survive. But what you do here is worse than any death."

Joe's shark eyes looked more puzzled than annoyed. "These creatures aren't sentient, Etty. Haven't you ever slapped at a mosquito? Stepped on a spider?"

Of course not. How could I? "When a fish is eaten in Wet—in the ocean—it becomes part of something larger, more powerful than itself. That is its destiny, its birthright. It deserves better than this. Better than you."

Joe studied me with those cold, shark eyes. My fingertips puckered, and I thrust my hands into my pockets. As if sensing my silent threat, Joe lowered his gaze.

"Time to take it apart, kids." Joe picked up the knife. "Etty, go find something else to do. We'll talk later about what you deserve."

* * *

I wandered the complex, merging with different schools as they flowed through the rooms and outdoor tanks, careful to stay slightly in the background, always out of reach. Humans marveled at the bleached bones of a gray whale, applauded the seals and sea lions that cavorted in small pools. They cheered the otters, lifting their young high onto their shoulders for a better view.

The same humans who would toss a fish onto a table and count how long it took to die. Truly, I would never understand you.

When the last human had straggled from the buildings and disappeared from view, I clambered down the cliff to the beach and stood before the waves.

For a moment I hated you, all of you, with a burning passion. These feelings, these experiences, were a part of me now and always would be, a slow poison I could not expel. The end could not come soon enough. I pictured the final wave pulsing forward, rising, crashing, enveloping Dryworld. In my mind I heard panicked shouts, the churn of machinery, the crash as buildings toppled. Then silence.

The tide surged forward, stopping just shy of my feet. My task seemed as insurmountable as swallowing a whale. Why persist? One step, and I could regain my true form. One step, and I could put all this behind me.

One step, and I would lose you forever.

* * *

I found you inside the lab office, surrounded by half-opened packages, staring at a computer screen. Images of fish swam across it, disappearing and reappearing once again. Homesickness swelled within me.

"How did it go with Joe?" Your smile seemed as forced as mine felt.

I perched on the edge of your desk, letting my human legs dangle as my hair billowed around me. "He sent me away."

You pursed your lips, blowing out air. "Not wise to get on Joe's bad side, Eight."

"Is there any other side?"

You chuckled as you lifted a thin film from one of the boxes. A loud pop sent me bounding to the floor.

"Relax, it's just bubble wrap." You handed me a sheet. "You put your thumb on one side, your finger underneath, and squeeze." Another pop, more subdued. "Try it."

I willed my hands to cooperate. "It's like squeezing seaweed bulbs."

"I know, right? Addictive." You shot me a sideways glance. "Ever do that where you're from? Squeeze seaweed?"

I spoke without thinking. Being in human form was affecting my brain. "Often. To strengthen our limbs for hunting."

A pause. "What kind of seaweed?"

You, too, had become suspicious.

"Are you asking where I'm from?"

You pointed at the map of Dryworld over your desk, the same map that hung on the wall above my aquarium. The map I had studied until I knew every mass, every bump that punctuated Dryworld. The map I had enveloped and shared with my wolf eel neighbor, pulse by pulse. That he, in turn, in signals even I could not understand, imparted to the vast, shifting consciousness of Wetworld.

"Can you show me your country?" you asked.

"Why? So you can check up on me?" My eyes watered. I quickly blinked the moisture away, not sure how it would affect the soft flesh beneath.

You lifted your hands as if to defend yourself. "Don't get mad. It wasn't my idea."

"Jane." I stared at the floor, shoulders hunched. This isn't over.

"Sarah, actually. She handles all Joe's paperwork. She needs to know what school you come from so they can scan your transcripts. You know, since all your luggage got lost."

At my blank look, you amended, "Or copy and mail them over. Whatever. So you can be here officially, you know—for real."

A chill coursed through me. "W-what makes you think I'm not real?"

Another chuckle. Despite my danger, I warmed to the sound. "Eight, of course you're real. Don't you want to get credit for the classes you take, and the work you do? And your stipend—you don't want to crash on my lumpy couch forever, do you?"

My hair flowed over my shoulders, hiding my face. My own personal cave. "I don't know what you mean. Where else would I stay?" I could not keep the tremor from my voice.

You patted my shoulder. If any of the others had reached towards me, I would have defended myself. Why did your touch not feel like a threat? Your palm on my flesh felt like nourishment, as if a part of me that had not required food could now never be satiated.

You smiled, and a little thrill shot up my spine. "Let's get something to eat, okay? It's been quite a day. We'll figure this out in the morning."

Relief washed over me. "Thank you."

"If you're not too tired, maybe we can hit a movie afterwards."

"A movie?"

You stopped so quickly we almost collided on the steps.

"Haven't you ever been to a theater?"

I improvised quickly. "There are no theaters where I live."

"Well, this will be an experience." You pulled out your phone and pressed some buttons, studied the screen. "Hey, I know where I'll take you. It's a little dated, not a first run place, but still fun. A restful end to an eventful day."

I fell into step beside you as we walked to your car. Our strides matched, as if the same currents guided us. Your words flowed over me like a new, clean wave, washing the stain of the day away.

* * *

After another meal of raw fish—you whispered something to the woman at the door, and she seated us far from the kitchens—we climbed back into the car. Exhausted by the day, lulled by the movement, my stomach satisfyingly full for the first time since I had transformed, I, who had rested with both eyes open my entire life until last night, once again fell wholly asleep.

"Eight, hey, wake up." Your fingers brushed my neck.

I was instantly alert. "I was not asleep," I lied. While Wetworld creatures constantly practice deception to eat and avoid being eaten, lying from shame was new to me.

"What's on your mind?" you said.

I jerked upright and clawed at my forehead, but felt nothing but smooth flesh. Your hand gently covered my own.

"It's an expression, Eight," you said. "Relax. There's nothing on your mind. It means, 'What are you thinking about?'"

A breath I did not even realize I was holding left my chest in a noisy exhale. I searched through the many layers of my mind, trying to remember my last thoughts before oblivion took me. "How well you keep within the lines while travelling. Because of this, I would expect you to have more regard for borders."

"Borders?" You did not seem angry, but genuinely interested. "You have to stay in one lane while driving, Eight. Otherwise you risk an accident."

"I understand. What I cannot fathom is why your respect for safety extends no further than obeying traffic signals."

Your gaze remained blank as you carefully steered down the street, then stopped at a red light.

"For example, the way you treat other nations," I continued. The light changed, and we moved forward.

You quirked an eyebrow. "I know our foreign policy is checkered, but compare us to any other primary power and we come out pretty well."

Even though I knew our discussion was futile, I could not let it go. "Think of the way you treat Wetworld! You obey no boundaries there."

Your eyes left the road to stare at me. "Wet what?"

"The oceans. As if they were there for you to plunder, and not an entity in their own right. To be respected as you would another country."

"We're working hard to change that, Eight. And we are making progress. If you look at what people were doing thirty, even twenty years ago—aerosols, pollution, overfishing. But this kind of change never happens quickly."

And now it is too late. I thought the words, but couldn't bring myself to say them.

"You have to reach out to the kids, change their perception," you continued. "That's why outreach, like the tours Sarah organizes, are so critical."

So intent was I on our discussion that I hadn't noticed the car had stopped. You walked around to my side and opened the door. The gesture made no sense. I was capable not only of opening the door, but ripping it from the vehicle. Yet I felt oddly gratified as you took my arm and steered me towards a large structure.

"Is that the theater?" The sight of figures milling around was comforting, a school of fish nosing a reef.

"No theaters, no restaurants." You shook your head. "Where did you grow up? In a cave?"

Your astuteness startled me. I smiled, and you squeezed my arm. Instead of reacting normally, I pressed even more closely against you.

"Well, a movie theater is an American icon—a symbol. Just like the flag is the symbol for the United States." You passed a shiny card to a young woman sitting behind a piece of glass, and she handed you two small pieces of paper. "Anyway, I hope you like it."

We slid through the outer cave into a dark inner chamber. My senses flared. This was as close as I had come to feeling at home since flopping out of my world into yours. This huge cavern, as subtly shadowed as home, lacked only the pressure of water, the faint scent of brine, to make crouching between shelves of rock seem natural.

You chuckled. "Not there, silly. We sit in the seats."

The chair collapsed beneath the pressure of your arm. I slid inside one, and you settled next to me. An air current so subtle as to be almost unnoticeable wafted scents our way; the sweaty smell of a human mingled with the odor of his prey. I twisted in my seat. Behind us, a large man thrust his hand into a container of salty gravel, then ingested it. The crunch resounded through the cavern.

"What is that smell?" I said.

"Popcorn. Want some? It's good."

I twisted again, sniffing, then pulled back, oddly disappointed. "I can't eat that."

You patted my arm. "A lot of people can't digest it. Would you like some candy, or a coke?"

You pointed to a different kind of container, which bubbled like a sulfur spring. I could not imagine ingesting it.

"No, thank you."

I squirmed in the seat, which did not allow for movement.

You slouched beside me, paying no attention to your surroundings. I wondered again what it would be like to live in such oblivion. No internal sonar always scanning, watching, gauging the depths and level of danger, how to meet it or avoid it; the dance of Wetworld. Those who survive learn to dance it very well.

And yet, if you did not extend your awareness to gauge the danger levels of your surroundings, what did you do with it? From what I had observed, humans tended to focus their awareness within, or on one another. Perhaps that accounted for your arrogance, your self-imposed blindness as Wetworld rose around you.

I peered at the floor, dark and stained and littered with a crumbly substance, not unlike a slick of sand after the tide had passed through. Damp, and sticky, but not wet. I pictured water pouring in through the back of the cave, coursing through the aisles. My limbs twisted to reach the welcoming tide.

"—the hell are you looking at?" The man seated behind me said, a snarl in his voice.

I jerked back, almost falling from my seat. This human body was getting its revenge, playing havoc with my senses. Before I could react, you spoke.

"She's a foreign exchange student, sir. This is her first movie." You squeezed my shoulder and pointed towards the front of the room. "Show's that way, Eight."

I peered through the gloom. "I don't see anything."

I turned around again, disliking the vulnerability of having humans so close by, yet out of my narrow field of vision. The man glared, his brow furrowed as if worms tunneled beneath his flesh. My forehead puckered in response.

"Can you tell your girlfriend to stop giving me the fish eye?"

You moved to the aisle, motioning me to follow. "What's going on, Eight?"

"I'm sorry." My head drooped, and I had to work hard to snap it upright. How did you manage to keep yourselves so rigid?

You leaned toward me, your breath warm in my ear. "That guy's kind of a jerk. Let's find seats further back."

I followed you, grateful for your perception. Yet, how could you possibly understand my unease? I had watched you move in and out of crowds all day, never giving a thought to where you were in relation to the people clustered around you. Why should you? No predators stalked you. Despite your physical weakness, you were the orcas of Dryworld.

Two seats at the back were empty. As we settled into them, a wave of darkness fell across the room, as if a whale glided above. I tensed.

"Relax, Eight. It just means the movie's about to start."

I molded myself to the seat, willing my heart to stop its erratic thumping. Before I could question you further, the wall at the front of the room brightened, as myriads of luminescent creatures fused together to create images.

"I know it's kind of corny, but since you've never seen it, and we're both marine scientists, I thought you might like it."

My human pulse quickened at the tale of a young mermaid who wanted to grow legs to roam Dryworld. I could have warned her that pretending to be something you are not carried unpleasant surprises.

After a while, I tugged at your sleeve. "She left Wetworld to mate with a human? That is her mission?"

The people in front of us turned around.

"What is the purpose? What offspring could they possibly have?"

"Shhh. We don't talk in the movies." I enjoyed the rush of your warm breath in my ear, savoring the feeling as the story unfolded like a bloom of seagrass. The cunning mollusk that sacrificed herself to save the foolish mermaid. The human who foiled her attempt and then destroyed her.

I realized that our missions were not so different, Ursula's and mine. To protect Wetworld, no matter the cost. The skin on my face grew moist. Would I, too, fail? Would I, too, be reviled, my mission misunderstood?

It took me a moment to notice that the room had lightened.

"So, what did you think?" you asked, as we walked from the theater into the night.

My mind was so flooded with images, it took me a while to reply. "Does this happen often? Ocean creatures camouflaged as humans?" Perhaps I was not the first to walk among you on human feet. My eyes scanned the sidewalk for a person whose gait did not quite match a biped form, or a gaze that seemed unnaturally watchful.

Your next words destroyed my hope. "Only in fiction, Eight. Not in real life." Your arm across my shoulders felt as familiar to me as my own. "Did you like the story?"

My hair drooped around my shoulders. "Octopi don't scheme like that. We improvise."

"You mean Ursula? She was a giant squid."

I searched my memory for what I had read in the marine lab. "They are both mollusks. Reclusive, not flamboyant. Cave dwellers. And we—they—do not move like that."

"I'd like to see your moves." A man's voice. Greasy, shoulder length hair, sharp teeth as crowded as a wolf eel.

You really wouldn't.

At my gaze, his lips tightened in a sneer. I calculated how much strength I would need to snap his backbone.

Before I could respond, I felt your internal force coalesce, like the luminous points on the screen. Your arm tightened around my shoulders.

"Lay off, okay? She's new here." Before the man could speak again, you pulled me away. "Predator."

I whirled to face you, aghast that you could sense my thoughts. "I would not have hurt him! I would have used my words!"

You laughed, equilibrium restored.

"Are you ever going to answer my question about the movie?" you said.

My heart thumped in my chest, and the corresponding pulse in my neck throbbed. Why was I so agitated? Yet, as if propelled by an underwater current, the words tumbled from my mouth. "Wetworld creatures look out for themselves. Survival is our—their—mission. Mollusks do not rescue foolish creatures who beach themselves."

You paused, jammed your hands into your pockets. "Ursula wasn't protecting Ariel. She wanted to destroy her."

"Destroy her?" When I had laughed before, I was imitating a sound I had heard around me. This time, true human mirth bubbled up from within. "Ursula tried to keep that silly girlfish from ruining her life. Even if it meant sacrificing herself in Ariel's place." I kicked at a pebble, which rolled off the curb into the street, bumping another pebble in its path.

Your gaze locked onto mine as if I was a fish, and you were trying to decide if I was poisonous.

"You're entitled to your opinion."

Your tone was devoid of all emotion, as if you had put up a wall in your mind and spoke from behind it. Even though I had not touched you, I sensed I had injured you in some way. That thought felt uncomfortable, like a piece of grit lodged in a tentacle.

I fell into step beside you. "Thank you for taking me to the theater, Matt. You knew what to expect from a movie. I did not. I'm sorry my thoughts are so displeasing."

You blinked, and your expression softened. "You're just a nonstop surprise, Eight. Here, we think the concept of true love is universal, that it transcends languages, cultures. That two beings as different as a prince and a mermaid can fall in love and, because of their courage and devotion, fortune smiles on them and they end up together. And then you come along and blow that perception all to hell."

Beneath the forced joviality in your tone, I could sense something deeper, something troubled. Your gaze met mine, and for a moment I felt as if you could see right through the deception that sustained me.

I studied your face, jaw jutting out like a piece of coral, eyes as green as water at its purest, when sunlight spilled through the surface and lightened the viscosity to a shimmering pearl.

My hand reached out and slid along your cheek, as smooth as seaweed—and nothing came between us, no shifting tides, no fronts of cool water, just my hand on your flesh, my gaze meeting yours.

My fingers found your lips, tracing their contours. Then they froze, as I remembered who I was, who you were, and that even the air I breathed was an illusion. More separated the two of us than if we were standing at opposite sides of the ocean.

My hand dropped. I noted how quickly, how cleanly it sliced through the air. Was this what made you so different from us? No pressure holding you in place, no currents to navigate. No need to think carefully before moving a limb, because to reveal one's location invited death.

But here in Dryworld, where danger did not lurk outside every cave, did not wait to pounce from behind each shrub…even the schools of chattering humans posed no threat. Like scavengers, you consumed dead prey, not one another. I could glide past any school of humans that I chose, dart into their midst and scatter them, and still I would be safe.

I took an experimental step from the curb into the street. Instantly you jerked me back. "You can't walk into the street without looking, Eight!" As if to illustrate your point, a vehicle roared past, inches from where I had just stood.

So I had gotten that wrong as well.

"Matt!" A voice called from behind us.

I jerked my head, forgetting the limitations of my neck. Jane and Sarah hurried forward, each shadowed by a stranger.

"Jane." Your voice lacked Jane's enthusiasm.

"What are you doing here? Oh." The "oh" was meant for me, as I moved from your other side. Jane's hand went to her neck, where the faint shadow of bruises showed from beneath her hair.

"I took Eight to a movie," you explained. "She's never seen one."

Sarah glanced at the marquee, quirked an eyebrow. "The Little Mermaid?"

You lowered your face, a sign that stood for shame. "Because it was about the ocean," I broke in. "Matt thought I would enjoy it." I sucked in a mouthful of air and told a new lie. "And I did, mostly. Even though it did not speak the truth."

Jane gave a mean-spirited laugh, and I realized something new— you postured as much with your speech as you did with your bodies. A sound could contain as many shades as a coral reef. Her voice turned sweet, with a poisoned edge. "Was it the animation that clued you in? Or that there's no such thing as mermaids? Or that crabs don't sing?"

My hair, alert to the danger of Jane's voice, stood on end. "A creature from Wetworld would not consort with the enemy. Not without a more significant purpose." Even as I said it, I wondered if it was true.

"Ariel didn't exactly consort with Ursula," Sarah began.

"Ursula was not her enemy. I meant the human."

"Prince Eric? But she loved him!" Jane seemed more agitated than the discussion warranted. "She gave up everything to be with him!" She stumbled slightly. Her escort laughed as he steadied her.

"Exactly. Her body, her voice," I had to think for a moment," her essence."

"But that's what people do when they fall in love, Eight." Sarah's tone was low, reasonable. "They change to please their soulmate. Because that's what love is. When you care about someone else's happiness more than your own."

"Even when that person—the soulmate—is slaughtering your people? Destroying your world?"

There was an uncomfortable pause. "Even fish eat other fish, Eight." You sounded perplexed.

"If they are quick enough, strong enough to catch them. But only to survive. They do not destroy entire populations, or make their world uninhabitable."

My tongue felt thick, the walls of my mouth swollen. Emotions made communication difficult.

Before Matt could reply, Jane put a hand on his arm.

"Hey, we're going dancing." She pointed to a flickering neon sign across the street. "Why don't you join us?"

You put your arm around my shoulders. "Maybe another time. Eight's had a long day."

"Very long," I agreed. "I need rest."

Jane tilted her head up at you, ignoring me. "So do I, but that's not stopping me. If you want to expose Eight to American culture, shouldn't she experience the real thing?"

She bared her teeth, more of a scowl than a smile. "C'mon, first round on me." She lifted her arms and gyrated her middle, then stumbled against her companion. His arm went around her waist, then dropped to caress her buttocks. You tensed.

"Looks like you're a few rounds ahead of us." You gave my shoulder a gentle squeeze, but your gaze was on Jane. Protective, like a seahorse guarding its young. "Eight, you up for it?"

Since I was awake and upright, I realized the question was rhetorical. I followed you across the street, careful this time to look both ways.

The new cave pulsed with so much sound it was impossible to hear. "What're you drinking, Eight? Saltwater?" Jane shouted. Before I could accept, she giggled, warning me of her trap.

"Water, please. But—without salt." No point in giving my treacherous limbs a chance to expose us.

"Oh, come on—don't tell us you don't drink? I heard all you Eastern Europeans put it away like breathing."

Again, you came to my aid. "She said water, Jane. You're drinking enough for both of you."

"Ain't that the truth." Jane motioned a waiter over.

"Water," she said again, mouthing the word as if was offensive. "So, Eight, how do you say water in whatever language you speak."

I took a deep breath and let it out slowly, as I had seen you do. "While I am here, I speak your language."

"And if I was there, how would I ask for water?" Jane clung to the subject like a barnacle. "What language do you speak, Eight?"

This time you did not help. In fact, you leaned forward, as did Sarah. My fingers twisted the paper napkin, tearing it in little shreds.

"Nuance." I said finally. It was the closest word I could think of. Sarah snickered.

Jane flushed. Had we been in Wetworld, I would have tensed in response. But whether to pounce or flee, I wasn't certain.

"What does that mean? Do you point at things? Read minds?"

"Hey, Jane, lay off." Your usually easy tone was tinged with something hard. "Anyone would think you're a Sociology major, not a marine scientist."

Jane leaned forward, nearly knocking over her drink. Your hand shot out to steady it. Her fingers closed over yours, full lips drawn into a pout. "You're the one who told her to use her words. I'm just trying to figure out what they are."

I gazed directly into Jane's eyes, but she did not flinch. "You might not like to hear them."

"Try me."

I chose my words carefully. "We use gestures more than words. To express emotions, we turn to color."

Before Jane could reply, Sarah broke in. "We do that too. Green with jealousy, red with anger, gray with shock."

"White with fear," you added.

Another similarity. It was as if unseen currents nudged us closer together, just when I needed to feel farther apart. Before Jane could press me further, you offered me your hand.

"Dance?"

I followed you to a patch of floor where humans twisted and writhed as if caught in a whirlpool. Two females tracked you with their eyes, gazes assessing. A low chuckle escaped my human lips as I understood what was happening.

"…funny, Eight?" I could barely hear you over the music, louder than incoming tide.

"They seek mates. And the music pounds like surf, rhythmic, relentless. It feels like home." The tears that had built up behind my eyelids chose this moment to release. I wiped them away with the cloth you had given me.

"Let's dance, then." You guided me into the midst of the dancers, posturing and gyrating your body. With a shock, I realized your display was meant for me.

An even greater shock was how my human limbs responded. I mirrored your movements, legs kicking, arms swinging. I closed my eyes and my body became one with the music, the heated air, the ebb and flow surrounding us. Like undulating through an empty kelp forest, no fear, no awareness.

Silence. I jerked to a stop.

"Lady, you can move." Your gaze was full of admiration as you led me back to our table.

My heart was hammering, skin flushed. Even while mating, we do no exert so much energy.

"Is this the first time you've gone dancing?" you said.

"I've never moved like this before." I flopped into my chair, then forced my limbs to straighten.

"D'you like clubbing?" Jane and her companion had returned from the dance floor. I reached for my water and sipped it, wondering why Jane was watching me so intently. The water tasted odd, but the frenzied movement had made me thirsty.

"I like the darkness." My tongue felt thick, and I paused to take another swallow. It didn't help. "But to move so swiftly, for so long? With no predators to flee from? It seems a needless expenditure of energy."

Jane giggled. "Oh, there's predators all right. But we dance so fast, they can't keep up."

"And if they can?" My words echoed oddly in my ears.

"We take them home." White teeth gleamed as Jane turned to face you. "And once we've taken what we wanted, we move on to the next fish in the sea. Isn't that how it works, Matt?"

Your gaze hardened. "Thanks for the invite, Jane, Sarah." You pulled out your wallet, and paper fluttered onto the table. "We're leaving. Next round on me."

Jane pouted. "I was hoping for at least one dance. Don't you remember—"

You cut her off. "Another time." Jane started to rise and you put your hands on her shoulders, easing her back into her seat. "Don't overdo it, okay? Joe's called a post-Open House meeting for nine tomorrow."

"But it's Sunday!"

"Like Joe cares," Sarah said. "He says the fish can't tell the difference."

"That is true." I was surprised at Joe's acuity. "Wetworld has no distinctions, like your calendar. Each day flows into the next."

Your lips brushed my ear. "Let's flow out of here before Jane makes a scene, okay?"

My steps felt unsteady, as if I'd misplaced a tentacle. Once outside, Dryworld seemed darker, more ominous. Quiet, except for the sonorous boom of seals calling to one another. I always found their cries ironic. The very sounds that indicates their safety alerts predators to their location.

Few people remained on the street. At home, I would know a shark was about to glide by, or a school of barracuda. I shivered.

"It gets cold when the fog rolls in." You pulled me close. I melted into your warmth, surprised at how peaceful I felt.

"You hungry?"

I shook my head. "I won't need to feed until tomorrow. Or the next day."

You shook your head. "You guys don't eat much, do you? Or drink. Or dance. Or go the movies. What do you do for fun?"

My limbs felt unsteady, and when I spoke, my words were slurred. "We observe. Hunt. And feed."

"That's all?" You sounded disappointed, as if I had missed something critical.

"It is enough."

Your hand stroked my hair, which lifted in response.

"And…do you fall in love?"

Love? Was that what I felt? Of all the emotions I had mimicked since my transformation, love remained elusive, like a small fish hiding in a reef, knowing its survival depended on stillness.

But what if that stillness was in itself a form of living death? No joy, no curiosity, no awareness of anything except the endless fight to survive. Thoughts tumbled through my head, thoughts I never could have conceived of in my true state.

I forced myself to answer. "We mate. Sire young, or bear them." I sighed, unable to remain indifferent to your hand, stroking, caressing. My hair wrapped itself around your palm, pulling it closer. "Occasionally, some survive."

"You have a high mortality rate."

I was having difficulty concentrating. My legs wobbled. I could not understand why. I had fed recently, so it was not hunger that made me weak.

"I feel…" I didn't know the word for this odd, unbalanced feeling. Entirely foreign, but not entirely unpleasant. It was as if boundaries I was not even aware of had melted away, leaving my mind as vast and echoing as the ocean. "Out of my depth."

Your breath was warm against my cheek. "You too, then? It's not just me?"

I shook my head, glad I was not alone.

"I didn't want you to think I was hitting on you, you know? You've got enough to deal with, culture shock, Joe, Jane." Your arms tightened around me. "But if you feel it too…"

The ground swayed. I leaned into you, glad of your support. "Most definitely."

Your lips brushed my forehead, my cheeks. My own pursed in response. I brushed them across your neck, with no thought but to return the pleasure that coursed through me. I could feel the vibration in your throat as you laughed. "Is that how Europeans kiss?"

"Kiss?"

Your arms tightened around me as your lips pressed against my own. And I, so swift that no predator could catch me, so skilled at camouflage that none could find me, did not hide or flee. It was as if I wanted to be caught, devoured. To become part of you.

Your breath became harsher as the kiss intensified. Heat seared my face and set my heart hammering in return.

In a searching, probing motion, your tongue slid between my lips like a hungry sea star. My sense of self-preservation flared. I jerked back, horrified. "You mean to eat me?"

A lone passerby snickered. Your face turned the color of rose coral. "Look, I'm sorry. I got carried away. Let's go back to my place. No funny business, I promise."

* * *

We did not speak as you drove to your cave. My head ached, my mouth felt stuffed with sand. In Wetworld, I would know I was dying. Here, I was not so sure. Frail as this human body appeared, it seemed remarkably resilient.

Once inside I sank onto your couch, grateful to conserve energy as you kicked off your shoes and placed your keys on a hook.

"Are you hungry? Thirsty?"

"Water. Please," I added, though asking instead of taking was a concept nearly as foreign as breathing air, or lingering in the open. "My head aches."

You leaned forward and sniffed at my breath, grimacing. "If it hurts now, just wait till morning." You handed me a glass and sat down beside me, scowling. "I can't believe Jane spiked your drink. I mean, I get why she could still be mad at me, but what a douche move."

I sipped the water, enjoying the sense of coolness. "Jane sees me as a threat," I said. "I understand her behavior. She is only human."

"You're very forgiving." You stretched your legs out onto the sofa table. The creatures in your aquarium strained forward. "Fish TV. Can't beat it." You gestured towards the tank. "I have seahorses, gobies, a pygmy angel, four kinds of coral…" your brow quirked as you stared at the tank. "Look how they're pressed against the glass. It's like they're watching us."

I sent a flash of energy, and the creatures dispersed.

You frowned. "Or not. Weird tides, odd fish behavior. I wonder if we're in for an earthquake?"

"Earthquake?"

"Do they have them where you come from? It's when the ground shakes really hard. Tectonic plates, you know?" You gave a worried glance at the living room window. "Our last big one was in '89. I was just a little kid, but I still remember it. It leveled downtown and caused a lot of damage. They told me that the marine lab got really messed up, too."

"I remember when that happened." Your forehead wrinkled, and I did a rapid time calculation. "Reading about it," I amended. "It changed things."

"How so?"

I closed my eyes, bringing up one of the scientific papers I had enveloped. "The elephant seals. Up until then, if a pup strayed from its mother, it usually died. Few elephant seals would nurse another's offspring. But after that earthquake, and the havoc it wreaked on the beaches, dams started to care for orphaned pups."

You nodded. "It created a big change in animal behavior. Unprecedented."

A thought formed in my consciousness, a glimmering of hope. I struggled to put it into words. "It was as if they understood that in order to survive they needed to change. If human actions caused a reaction that threatened the species, could you alter your behavior to avoid extinction?" I did not realize I had grasped your hand until your fingers went rigid beneath mine.

"Is there something we need to talk about, Eight? Something you folks are doing off the grid that has global implications?" Gone was the relaxed, kindly mentor. Now I faced a keen-eyed scientist.

I knew I should stop talking, but my tongue ignored my silent command. "If an aggressive species meets another species, one that is stronger, more capable, and does not retreat..."

Something behind your eyes relaxed. "You mean niche differentiation?"

I tried again. "In the ocean, creatures maintain a balance that allows all to survive. Could you do the same?"

You cocked your head, forehead wrinkled as you considered my question. Were you an octopus, I would be able to tell your thoughts by the colors coursing through your body. Now, I could only wait.

"Americans? Or the human race?" You patted my hand, and I realized you were trying to reassure me. "I wouldn't worry too much about humans, Eight. Besides viruses...and maybe Joe...we're still at the top of the food chain."

"Maybe not for much longer."

I didn't realize I'd spoken aloud until your back stiffened. "I meant, you never know what could suddenly disrupt your ecosystem," I said hastily. "Something you never conceived of as a threat can still prove deadly, if it strikes without warning."

I bit my tongue. I had said too much.

I need not have worried. You understood my panic, but mistook my meaning. "Sounds pretty dog-eat-dog where you come from." Your fingers traced the contours of my cheek. "Over here you can relax a little bit, you know? Jane will mellow out eventually, Joe's counting the days till his next trip, and then you can work on your research without stressing about stuff."

You gave me another sideways glance. "So what is your focus?"

Preserving Wetworld.

I drifted to the window and gazed out into the street. In Wetworld, we live in the moment; past and future are not in our consciousness. But this human mind was envisioning things that did not yet exist; waves pummeling the shoreline, waters rising, cars floating, streetlights cracking as the force of the tides snapped them like seaweed bulbs. Humans swept away, screaming, as terrified as the fish in Joe's bucket. And then, peace, as Wetworld restored itself.

But at what cost?

Another new sensation washed through me. Remorse.

Did it really have to end this way?

On the sofa, you waited for my answer.

"I was sent here to accomplish one thing, but now, I wish to attempt another." Confusion swirled through me like tide through a pool, giving, taking, renewing. Was it possible, to create a balance with Dryworld? Were they capable of compromise? Were we?

I clamped my lips shut, terrified I would blurt out my mission. I needed your help—craved it—but even in my present form, human skin prickling with sweat, human emotions threatening to overwhelm my thoughts, I knew this could never happen. I took refuge in pretended confusion, but sadly my thoughts had never been more clear.

"I—I can't talk about it. Not now."

"Tired? It's been a day, huh?"

You laughed at my puzzled expression. "I forget how many figures of speech we use without thinking. I meant, it's been a long day."

I grew suddenly wary. Was this another attempt to expose me? "The length of your days does not vary. Only the light to dark ratio within."

Another chuckle. "It means, a tiring day. A busy one."

You leaned back, hands clasped behind your neck. Such a trusting posture. "So, what would you like to study? If it gets approved?"

Words slipped out without filters. "I want to learn all about you."

"Westerners? I'm sure you'll pick up our culture while you're here. Watch some TV, surf the net. You're smart. You'll soak it up like a sponge."

"That is not what sponges do." I came closer and traced the lines on your forehead, feeling them smooth out beneath my touch. "Not Westerners. You."

"Are you sure, Eight?"

I nodded, not trusting myself to speak.

You put your arms around me, and I pressed myself against you. Up until now, one concept had governed my world. Live or die. Eat or be eaten. Envelop, or become enveloped.

But this connection—merging, not consuming—was as hard to grasp as an additional dimension. Could we do this? Create an understanding, a bridge that spanned two worlds? Perhaps Dryworld was more than the threat we perceived. Perhaps, in some inexplicable way, it was linked to our own survival. Not just survival, but evolution. All of a sudden, my mission made sense. All for one and one for all…was it possible? Had I arrived in time?

In time to save Wetworld. Just. The wolf eel's voice sounded sluggish, weary.

I looked out the window and imagined the tide running along the road, slapping at the windows until it forced its way in. I thought of the fishes in the lab, watching me struggle, sharing their essences.

Arguing was futile, but I did anyway. *There is more here than you know. More than you see.*

I see Wetworld renewed, or destroyed. Which will it be?

Your fingers traveled across my neck, my face, bringing me back to the present. "Eight? Are you sure?"

I gasped, thinking for an absurd moment that you had heard my thoughts. But as you kissed the insides of my arms, you were clearly thinking of something else.

Thought fled as this human body responded to your kisses, your caresses. New sensations coursed through me, each more intense than the last. In Wetworld, we know hunger, fear, pain, satiety. These feelings keep us alive. But I had no words, no concepts, for the emotions that overwhelmed my consciousness, the shudders that had nothing to do with survival.

After a while, you spoke. "Do you have protection?"

"From you?"

You chuckled. So many nuances to human laughter. Sadness overwhelmed me at the thought of that sound extinguished forever.

"You know, are you on the pill?"

I did not feel anything beneath me, but reached down and swept my hand across the cushion. I felt only the seat of the couch, warm and wrinkled from the heat and weight of this human form.

"I don't feel any pills," I told you.

You laughed and propelled me down the hallway, into a cave that must be your own. I could smell you, feel your essence as you settled me on the bed.

You opened the drawer of the bedside table. "I'm sure I've still got something." You pulled out a shiny square, then looked down at me, your eyes serious.

"Eight, you sure about this? No pressure—you can stay here until we find you a place. We don't need to take this any further, you know? It's totally up to you."

Your words rolled over me like a warm front, though I had no idea what you were saying.

I rested my hand against your bare chest, felt your flesh beneath my fingers, the beat of your heart, the pulse of your blood. Your throat vibrated beneath my touch.

"We are not so different, you and I," I told you.

"We are in the ways that matter," you murmured against my neck, and then you showed me.

In Wetworld, mergings are brief; they must be, as both mates are especially vulnerable during the act of procreation. But this exchange of sensation, this synergy of pleasure…my human mind spun out of my grasp as you led me through the shallows, beyond the depths.

Afterwards, we lay together, the light from the bedside clock like a tiny phosphorous glimmer peeking out from a reef. I stirred, and you turned towards me, nothing between us, as if the atmosphere had disappeared and nothing separated us from one another. Illusion, yes—but one I craved so badly that when you reached for me again, I did not resist. I simply wanted more of you. The concept of taking more than one needed was a human practice I suddenly understood with complete clarity.

You made this merging playful, a pair of frolicking dolphins. Once again we rose to dizzying heights, before all boundaries dissolved and we grasped one another, gasping and entwined.

You reached for a piece of my hair and rubbed it between your fingers.

"That was awesome," you murmured.

For once, we were in complete agreement.

You gave my hair a gentle tug before releasing it. "But I don't think I'll ever really understand you."

I fell back against the pillows, spent. I agreed with that too.

For a long while I watched you sleep, mesmerized by the rise and fall of your chest, the rhythmic sound of your breathing. I knew it was time to return home. But despite my mission and everything that depended on it, I could not wish you harm. I wanted to protect you, as you had protected me from the moment you caught sight of me at the entrance to my cave, and continued to do so even as I struggled to comprehend where I was, what I had become.

Lying beside you as the sky lightened, I knew what I must do. I eased myself out of your bed, slipped out the door, and let the scent of Wetworld guide me.

* * *

"Jane, calm down. I can't understand you."

Startled, I bolted upright. Had I slept like that in Wetworld, I never would have woken. Sunlight streamed through the window, sending sparks of light throughout your cave. You stood beside the bed, phone jammed to your ear. "Deep breaths, okay? What happened?"

Your lips creased into a frown. "Yeah, I get it." Your gaze slid past me to the door, then back again. "Yeah, she's here. Not that it's any of your—"

Jane's voice shrilled from your phone, tinny and excited, but I couldn't make out her words.

I followed your gaze down the hall, seeing the wet, sandy splotches in front of the door. What had I done? I had meant to return for a moment only, to gaze at you one last time before losing you forever. Instead, I had fallen asleep. This human body had gotten its revenge.

I scrambled to my feet. You gestured for me to remain still as you spoke into your phone.

"Sit tight, Jane. I'll head over and we'll see what's going on. Calm down, okay?"

You turned to me, eyes troubled. Gone was all the warmth from last night. You smiled, but with your lips only. "Good morning."

I glanced out the window, but the day looked no different than the one before. "Why?"

You had reached out to stroke my hair, but your hand dropped to your side at my question. "You're right," you said. "Maybe not so good. That was Jane. I need to head to the lab."

"Why?" I repeated.

"I'm not sure. Jane's there now. She's really upset. Something about a break in, fish missing…" Your gaze fell to the floor, splotched with drying bits of sand. When you turned back, your eyes looked different, guarded. "I'd better check it out. Before Joe comes in, you know?"

I had not expected this. I thought the lab would be deserted today. The eel—Aunt Martha—could not be disturbed. "Jane is at the lab? Doesn't the sign on the door say, 'Closed Sunday'?"

"We're closed to the public on Sundays, Eight. But our specimens need to be fed and monitored every day." You pulled on your pants and a sweater, still avoiding my eyes. "Wait here, okay? Catch up on your sleep. I won't be long."

"Humans—people can't be in the lab, Matt. Not today." I knew you wouldn't understand, but I had to try. "Tell Jane she must leave. At once."

You studied me as if I was a specimen again. "So you noticed it yesterday, didn't you? Something up with Martha? That's what Jane said." Your eyes narrowed. "Do you know anything about this, Eight?"

Everything. But I shook my head, mimicking one of your more useful gestures.

You bent to kiss me, hesitated, then straightened again. "I'll be back as soon as I can." The door clicked shut.

For a long while I just sat there, my mind reeling, the bitter taste of failure in my mouth. I stared at one of my hands, wondering just how long the illusion would hold before it collapsed into a tentacle. How long I could survive in your atmosphere. When you found my shriveled carcass on your return, would you understand? When the giant wave broke, would you know I was responsible?

Then, faintly in the back of my mind, the eel's voice. Come back.

The lab took longer to reach in daylight, with so many more humans about. Roads I had travelled hours ago yesterday were now filled with water. Wetworld sucked at them greedily, clamoring for more. A woman snatched her spawn from a carrier moments before a wave washed it away.

Finally I reached the beach at the edge of the marine lab complex. I wiped the spray from my cheeks. The ocean reached out to me, soaking through my skin, awakening my true self. I clenched my fists, willing it back. My stride lengthened as I hurried towards the lab. Wetworld could not claim me yet.

Matt was the key. I would explain everything to him—who I was, what I was. He must answer for Dryworld, bargain for his world as I did for mine. Between us, we could—we must—restore the balance.

The tide reached forward, tickling my toes. The eel's voice again, an agonized whisper. Too late.

Heart pounding, breath harsh in my lungs, I moved faster than I had ever moved, even in my true form, the salty froth stinging my heels. I yanked the office door open and slipped inside. The tide crashed against it, water pouring through the sides and pooling on the floor.

I dashed through into the tank room. The row of aquariums glowed softly in the darkness, the harsh lights within illuminating their emptiness.

But something had changed since my nocturnal visit. The wolf eel's tank stood empty, cave overturned, water still and dark.

Panic seized me. "Matt!" I dashed through the tides, peered in the windows, but I knew where I would find you.

I entered Joe's lab and stood against the door, panting. You and Jane stood over the dissection table, your bodies obscuring the contents.

Jane turned and saw me. Her voice sounded as high and shrill as a baleen whale. "What is she doing here?"

You glanced at me from the corner of your eye, gloved hands clasped around something long and dark. "I asked you to wait at home, Eight. I know how hard this part is for you."

I pushed my way through you to the table. My insides went cold. Aunt Martha lay still in your hands. I closed my eyes and reached out, and he sent a flicker of consciousness my way, like an errant air bubble. I sensed pain, and fear, and underneath that, regret mingled with excitement.

Change was coming, and the eel would not live to see it. I pictured the wave swelling, breaking, destroying everything. For a moment, I envied him.

Your gaze fell to the watery trail behind me. "Have you been tide-pooling, Eight? Probably not a good idea, with these weird fluctuations. The tides seem to be rising by the minute."

"What have you done?" I sent my awareness towards the eel, willing it to live for a few moments longer. No flicker of consciousness met mine. I leaned against the table, all strength drained from this human frame.

"What is wrong with you?" Jane said.

Instead of answering her, I stared at you. How could I have been so mistaken? "You told me you rescued this creature from cruelty. You told me you cared about Wetworld, about her creatures. And now you…you…"

"All of them were gone when Jane came in this morning, Eight. Except for a dead wolf eel. This is an autopsy, not murder. Martha started going downhill right after the Open House. You noticed it too. We need to find out why."

I backed away, my sides heaving as all my hopes collapsed around me. "He is not dead. He is conserving energy."

"That makes no sense." Jane's eyes narrowed. "If you'll just leave us alone, some of us have real work to do."

The sight of the eel, limp and pale against the cold steel table, caused an odd flutter in my heart. Your scalpel had sliced him from beneath the gills to the tip of his tail.

You had gone too far, this time. Too far for the eel to recover. Too far for me to intercede. From beyond the walls I could sense the ocean swelling, waves gathering.

You reached out, then drew your gloved hand back. Blood and scales dripped from it. "Hey, I'm sorry you had to see this, Eight. We all have our favorites. Why don't you wait in the office? We're almost done."

Ignoring you, I ran my human finger along the eel's scales. Now I understood the heightened sense of urgency, the odd flutter in the center of my being. The rasp of dry air in my lungs. Without Aunt Martha's strength to bind the essences that maintained this form, how much time did I have left? Time. A concept that has so little meaning in Wetworld meant everything now.

But the eel wasn't dead. Not yet. Or my false form would already have dissolved around me.

I tugged the scalpel from your hands and nudged the flesh aside. Jane gasped as the now-exposed heart gave a slow pulse. A long pause, then another. And another.

"It pulls its essence within," I explained. "That's how it renews itself, survives the brackish medium you keep it in."

"That's—impossible!" Jane set down her scalpel and stared at me, as if I had somehow resuscitated the eel. Aunt Martha's heart began to beat faster.

Over the roaring in my ears, I heard you exhale. "I'm so sorry, Eight. I didn't realize. But maybe this can help, at least for a little while." You put down your scalpel and turned away, rummaging through the cupboards.

"I don't know, Matt." Jane's voice was hesitant. "That seems even more cruel. He'll suffer." Jane's scalpel poised over Martha's heart. Wouldn't it be better—"

"No!" My tentacles—fingers, still—wrapped around her wrist. "He needs to live as long as possible. It's critical."

"I hate it when your hair does that. It's creepy." But Jane tossed her scalpel into the sink.

You turned towards us, a tube in your hand.

"Glue?" So I could still read.

"To patch small wounds." You ran a seam across Martha's side, then gingerly tapped the skin back together, sealing the gash. "It won't hold forever—it's water resistant, not waterproof—but it might give him a little more time."

"Not enough," I said, finding it difficult to form words. I choked, hands against my mouth, gasping. Holes formed inside me, and I could picture Wetworld gushing through them. I fought to hold it back, knowing it was useless, but unable to concede. "We must put him back in his tank. He'll live a while longer. Perhaps a few hours, perhaps a day. When his heart stops beating, you'll know."

"How?" Jane said. "I mean, I found it—him—floating."

My mouth tingled. Inside cold lips, my tongue began to swell. Because this human form will dissolve around me.

"You'll know," I repeated.

As if sensing my desperation, you quickly lowered the eel into a bucket of water. Jane and I followed you to the tank room, where you tipped Martha back into his aquarium. Once inside, Aunt Martha slowly righted, staring at us through the glass. But more separated us than air and water. Before I could reach out, Martha righted himself and tried to swim, clumsily bumping the sides, seeking an exit that did not exist.

But alive, at least for the moment. Hope flared within me, only to dissolve like waves upon the beach as I looked at Martha's struggling form.

You reached towards me, but your hand dropped before it touched mine. The world swelled between us, pushing us apart. The temperature remained the same, but cold swept through me. The skin on my hands began to loosen, jell. I crammed them into the pockets of the sweatshirt jacket you had lent me, the one that said, "Make friends with anemone," across the front. I longed to tell you that I finally understood irony.

"I'm truly sorry, Eight. I didn't realize."

I wanted to tell you that it wasn't relevant, that all that mattered was for you to flee as far inland as you possibly could. Before I could speak, you held up your hand, a signal to listen. Joe's car pulled up in front of the building. The door slammed. He splashed through the parking lot and up the steps.

We trudged into the office to meet him.

"Joe, the meeting isn't for another hour," you said. "We're just sorting some stuff out."

Joe pointed at me, fingers shaking. "You."

You moved between the two of us, protecting me yet again. But I was not the one who needed protection.

"All our research, years and years, ruined." Joe's form quivered with rage. "Why, Etty? It's not like your lab can steal our credit. Not from prison, which is where you're going."

I looked out the window at the ocean, felt it gather, felt the tide flood my human veins. How could you not be aware of what was happening?

"Credit? You think you deserve credit for torturing Wetworld creatures?"

Your arm fell across my shoulders. "Sir, that's a big accusation. Do you have proof?"

Joe's gaze was as cold as the Arctic Sea. "Jane synced her phones to the security cameras." He glared at me. "She didn't trust you. Looks like she was right."

The look in your eyes when you turned to me was more painful than a barracuda's teeth.

"Eight. I thought we were friends—maybe more than friends. How could you do this to us?"

Like a wave that had risen, built, and released towards the shore, I could not stop myself. "Dryworld explodes like an algae bloom, wiping everything out. We tried to work with you. We rose slowly. A warning. Heated, nudged icecaps aside. But you did not change. You had to be stopped."

Joe loomed over me. "Stopped? Stopped from what?"

You stepped between us. "Joe, I don't think she means what it sounds like. The language barrier, you know? Let me take her home and we'll go through a dictionary. About the lab animals, Eight did a terrible thing, releasing them. I can't understand why. But I'll work with her to make things right."

But Joe, whose shrewd gaze saw more than yours, my love, was not to be placated. He understood that something had shifted, that the threat I presented was real, even if he still had no clue what it really was.

"Do you know how much trouble you'll be in for interfering with our specimens, Etty?"

"I was not the one who interfered with them. I merely put them back where they belonged."

"Prison is where you belong. I'm calling the police. Matt, stay with her until they get here." Joe stalked away.

The pounding tide hummed through my limbs. My human arms thickened, the flesh coarsening, puckering on the underside. I could tell you sensed something amiss. Beneath the illusion of flesh, suckers formed. In the dry atmosphere, they itched unbearably.

"All our hard work—wasted." Your eyes grew cold, and I felt something I had never felt from you before. Judgment. Absurd, I know, but your gaze wounded me more than had you bitten me at the base of my neck. That would bring only oblivion. This brought a wash of unpleasant emotions, as if you had taken a coral branch and stirred my insides.

"I had to protect the creatures of Wetworld. Before you destroyed us all. That is why I transformed."

Your eyes clouded with doubt. "You mean you became one of those rabid animal rights activists? Let me haul you through a kid's cancer ward at the hospital, and then you can tell me what we do here is wrong!"

How had I ever thought you could understand? A cramp tore through my middle, and I doubled over, gasping.

"Right or wrong," I wheezed, "it is over."

And it was. If my illusion could have been enough to unite our worlds, if I might have somehow persuaded you to halt the disaster Dryworld hurtled toward, perhaps keeping Martha alive might have given me time to reach out, to plead for you.

But my human shape was not the true deception. The true illusion was hope, that Dryworld and Wetworld might grow to understand and respect one another, to create an understanding. A bitter taste filled my mouth as I finally understood.

My legs twisted beneath me. Suddenly unable to stand, I dropped into your chair. My muscles seized, contracted. It wouldn't be long now. "Matt, listen to me. I must explain—"

"Don't pay her any attention," Jane snapped. "I don't care what she says, there's no excuse for what she did." She put her hand on your arm. You did not shake it off.

Your eyes narrowed. "If you have any more surprises, Eight, share them now."

I searched this human brain for words you could comprehend. "When I followed you to your home…" I was panting now, your atmosphere turning to poison within my body.

"You mean to his apartment?" Jane again, her spite undiminished.

"No. From my cave to your side of the ocean. Dryworld."

"What are you talking about?" Jane's voice reflected her disbelief.

"Just listen. There isn't time for anything else. After I followed you here, I began to understand you. You, and Jane, and Sarah. Even Joe." My hands twisted together, an oddly human gesture.

You sat down hard, the chair squeaking a protest. Jane stood behind you, her eyes on the doorway.

"I learned that humans are more than a pestilence to be destroyed. You are part of the same balance that upholds Wetworld."

Gills strained beneath my too-soft flesh. I took a slow breath, wondering how many more breaths I would be able to tolerate of your atmosphere. "I came here last night to convince Wetworld not to follow through with their plan. To explain that your survival is critical to our own.

"The wolf eel understood. But without him to communicate with Wetworld, to persuade them…" My arms went slack, the sleeves of your jacket hanging loosely from my shoulders.

I pointed towards the window, where a rising fringe of spray filled the glass. You stared at the waves battering the shoreline for a long time, each larger, more powerful than the one before.

When you turned back to me, your face was as gray as the tide. "Eight, did you hit your head? You're not making any sense. You glanced at Jane. "What did you put in her drink last night?"

"Let her finish, Matt." Jane stepped closer, but cautiously, the way a shark might circle prey to see if it still posed a threat.

You shook your head. "Call 911. Something's wrong with her."

"Now you notice."

Before Jane could punch in the numbers, I reached out with an arm that had lengthened, thickened, and knocked the phone from her hand. It crashed to the floor and spun beneath your desk.

"You crazy bitch!" Jane knelt down to retrieve her phone. It would take nothing to reach out and wind my arm around her waist, squeeze her in half. I stopped, aghast. Wetworld creatures feed or flee. We do not retaliate. Vengeance was endemic to Dryworld. I had absorbed more humanity than I realized.

"I'm glad you're going to prison," Jane spat. "You deserve it."

"Prison?" Even though every second was precious, I gripped the side of your desk and hoisted myself upright. "Like the Wetworld creatures you captured, tortured? What right did you have to take them?"

Jane stepped forward, her face inches from mine. "Because we can."

My lungs burned. How long can a mollusk live out of water? I was about to find out.

"So if I can do this…" My arm flopped free from the jacket sleeve.

Jane's eyes nearly rolled up in her head as my fingers swelled into tentacles. They lengthened, caressed her chin, then wound around her neck.

"It is acceptable for me to hurt you? Destroy you? Because I can?" My tentacle tightened.

"Matt!" Jane squeaked, her eyes impossibly wide. "This is what she did to me in the touch tank! Make her stop!"

"Eight!" The shock in your voice mirrored the confusion in your eyes. "I don't know who the hell you are, or what you think you're doing. But I need you to use your words. You promised."

I jerked my limb away, cramming it back into the sleeve.

Jane collapsed to her knees, her face a rictus of terror. "Matt—she's a monster!"

"Go home, Jane," you said, without taking your eyes off me. "I'll stay with Eight until the police come."

Jane paused at the door. Our eyes met, and I could see terror warring with jealousy. Her hand brushed her throat, where a series of new bruises decorated her flesh. Her gaze went from me, to you, to me again, to the hair flowing around my shoulders, the strands thickening and twining around me. Gills strained for my throat to open. My three hearts thudded as I gulped for breath. Not yet.

"Who are you?" she demanded. Her gaze swiveled to you. "Ariel, come to claim your prince? Because Matt will never, never belong to you!"

"Ursula," I croaked. "Here to protect my realm. From you."

My true self burst through the human form, tearing apart my fragile garments, spilling onto the floor.

"It's n-not possible." Jane's hand gripped the doorway. "I'm hallucinating. You drugged me. Is this payback for what I did to your water at the bar? Because it isn't funny."

You spoke in a tone I had never heard. "You're not hallucinating, Jane."

"Get in your car and drive, as far away from the shore as you can. Before…you can't," I rasped. But Jane was already gone, leaving only screams behind her.

My neck felt stiff and swollen as I turned towards you. I stretched out a hand—no longer a hand, but not entirely a tentacle. You recoiled, your face a mask of horror. "I am so sorry, Matt. This was not how— what—" I stopped. Explaining seemed as daunting as a salmon's journey upstream. Yet, like the salmon, I had no choice but to try.

"We had to stop you. Before you destroyed our home, destroyed us all. But before we could do that, we had to…"

My body swelled, collapsing onto your feet. By some freakish miracle, my head remained human. I waited for you to kick me aside, to run away. But you just sat there, staring.

"Stopped—how? What are you planning to do? Scare us to death?"

I shook my head, the movement slow and painful. "Last night, I reached out to Martha. I explained that despite your wanton destruction, you had something to offer us. I asked—begged—him to reason with Wetworld, to give you more time."

"And I'm talking to a mollusk," you muttered.

Our eyes met, and once again, you were talking to me.

"Are you saying the ocean sent you as an emissary, asking us to stop polluting, overfishing, melting the ice caps?"

You crouched on the floor beside me, your eyes more sad than frightened. "People won't stop, Eight. If they knew that, what do you call it—Wetworld creatures could shape shift like some freaking science fiction movie, they'd kill you faster. It wouldn't be The Little Mermaid, it'd be War of the Worlds.

"Which is why we must stop you."

"How? With all due respect, you have a big disadvantage. You can't breathe on land. Unless others of your kind—"

You jerked around, as if expecting more octopi to ooze through the walls.

I spoke through cracked lips. "Actually, we have a huge advantage. We can breathe underwater. And this planet—-our planet—is three quarters water." I pointed a tentacle towards the window, where a wave towered in the distance. "Wetworld is rising."

"That's preposterous! Fish don't control the oceans!"

I waved towards the map on the wall. The same as the map above the tank. The map I had studied, absorbed—cut my teeth on, you humans would say. The map that showed icecaps melting, tides shifting, waters rising.

"You started the changes," I said. "Through myriads of small electrical impulses, connecting, amplifying, Wetworld can intensify them."

Stunned as you were, you still didn't believe me. "Fishes and marine mammals are instinct driven. They don't influence evolution."

"Even instinct-driven creatures can change their behavior, in response to a threat." I replied. "Just like the elephant seals."

You leaned closer. Even as my true form claimed me, I felt no desire to streak away.

"But what about us?"

Your question echoed in the vastness.

I fought to form the words. "Us, as in you and me?" From the way my hair had slicked back into my brain, and from the tentacles bursting through my skin, it must have been as clear to you as it was to me that there never was an 'us.' Not really.

"'Us' as in people. Humans."

And with those words, the bridge between us shattered. I saw myself through your eyes, a monster, a freak. A threat.

What was left of my human voice trembled as I spoke. "That depends on you, Matt. Wetworld creatures respond. We do not aggress. If you halt your destruction of the atmosphere, and the oceans, we will stop rising."

I lifted a tentacle towards the window, now covered with sea foam. Beyond it, the deadly wave continued to grow.

Your head drooped. "If your plan was to destroy humanity all along, why did you bother to infiltrate us first?"

In a language not my own, using concepts I barely understood, I struggled to make you understand. "Wetworld creatures do not destroy. We envelop. Predator and prey become one. Before we could neutralize the threat you pose, we needed to envelop you. To give you a chance to continue, even if as part of something else. So your essence can survive."

Shock widened your eyes, turned your skin pale. I waited for a death blow. Perhaps a kick to the head, my most vulnerable part. You would know this.

Instead, you surprised me all over again.

"Eight. Please. Help us." Your fingers, soft as seaweed, brushed against my neck.

Your caress, so unexpected, wrenched me back into human awareness. I sensed the wave through your eyes, the horror, the panic.

"That tsunami will kill me, Eight. It will kill everyone. Men, women, animals, children. Babies. You lived among us, Eight. We were…intimate. Is this what you want? What Wetworld wants? Mass murder?"

Again, irony. You, who systematically destroyed our species, our environment, for your own gain, who devour our denizens in alarming quantity, could not stomach the tables turning.

Despite all of that, I could not countenance destroying you.

I reached out to the wolf eel, dormant in his cave.

Give them time to survive. Or we are no better than they are.

It changes nothing.

I looked into your eyes, saw Dryworld through them one last time.

It changes everything.

My breath burned as we stared at the window. Slowly the wave subsided, its deadly swell absorbed by the water beneath.

The wolf eel's essence wavered, vanished.

"How did you do that?" you said. "Did Wetworld change its mind?"

The skin beneath my shirt cracked and curled away. My neck felt stiff and swollen as I shook my head. "The eel slowed the first wave. To give us time."

"Time to warn people? To get away?"

"To say goodbye."

With a weary sigh, I collapsed at your feet. My lungs gave a painful squeeze. I twisted, fighting the gravity that had taken hold. My gaze fastened on yours, and a trickle of saltwater ran down my cheeks. And I realized that, even if these were my last moments of consciousness, I would rather spend them gazing at you than doing anything else.

My vision blurred. My flesh was rapidly drying. As soon as my lungs transformed, it would be over.

You scooped me up in your arms. More saltwater splashed upon my head. I took my last breath…

And then my first, as you slipped me inside—not my glass cage, but something smaller, darker. A bucket filled with seawater. From its smell, it came from my aquarium.

I heard you talking on your phone, your tone urgent. Then car doors slamming, and footsteps sloshing through the yard.

"Where is she?" Joe's voice boomed through the walls. "Jane told me what she did. But she also said some crazy stuff about Eight growing tentacles, attacking her?"

Your laugh sounded forced. "I wouldn't put too much credence in that part of her story. You know what students are like. She was out drinking last night pretty late."

"Why didn't you keep Etty here?" Joe demanded.

"I tried. She's very dangerous. Unpredictable. Jane wasn't wrong about that."

"She's freakin' crazy!" Joe snorted. "Why did you ever allow her into my lab in the first place? Couldn't you tell she was nuts?"

"With all due respect, sir, *you* invited her. But we have a bigger issue." You pointed towards the ocean. "A tsunami is coming. Possibly the first of several. I've alerted the Coast Guard, local news stations. We need to evacuate before it's too late."

A growl, then more orders barked into Joe's cell phone. "Have Sarah fill out a restraining order until we catch her and deport her," he told Matt. "I don't want that maniac within a mile of my lab. Who knows what she'll decide to do next?"

"I don't think that will be a problem, sir. I got the feeling this was the last place on earth she'll ever come back to."

I shrank into myself, held as still as possible inside the tiny bucket. Soon I would run out of oxygen. It was just as well, I realized. For the first time in my existence, death seemed preferable to survival.

"Why don't you head inland, sir? I'll lock up and follow you."

"Foreigners." More sloshing, then a car door slammed. As the sound faded into the distance, your face appeared above the bucket. I stared at you, willing myself to store your features in my mind.

"Can you still understand me?" you whispered, even though we were alone.

I wiggled a tentacle.

"Look, I don't know how it works down there in—what do you call it? Wetworld. But some of us are trying our best. At heart, we're no different than you. We all just want to survive. It's harder on land— more complicated."

The water in the bucket slopped back and forth and I realized you had picked it up. What would you do with me? The thought of that cold steel table flashed through my mind. My flesh contracted as if it could already feel the scalpel slicing through it.

Or, if you survived, perhaps you would take me to a new aquarium, somewhere safe for the moment, on higher ground. In time, you would forget me. I would watch as other women sat beside you, touching, kissing, merging…

I preferred the scalpel.

A new sound, and a new smell—the fresh, clean scent of a tide pool.

You set the bucket down. "If what you say is true—if you really came here to envelop us—then perhaps you'll envelop this." You tipped the bucket, allowing me to glide into the water. "Mercy."

You squatted down and put your hand into the water. I wrapped a tentacle around your wrist, as if that futile gesture could keep us together.

A wave crashed into the tide pool. As it wrenched me away, I knew a new feeling, something that would stay with me forever. My legacy from Dryworld. The aftermath of love. Yearning.

* * *

Wetworld is quiet. The blaring of horns, the jangling, pulsing cacophony of your world has been replaced by gentler sounds. My mind grows peaceful again. Life is simple—hunt, eat, rest, hunt again.

Until I think of you. And then, it all comes back in a rush like a crashing wave.

I remember flashes of a different creature, with flowing hair that seemed alive. A creature that laughed and danced, read and dreamed. As much as she was capable of, loved.

Humor. Irony. Despair. I savor the words, the concepts, beneath my tongue, molding them, tasting them.

There is more to your world than to ours, my love, more shadings, more complexity. I understand why you cannot stop yourselves, why you cannot shift from this path.

Do you understand why we cannot shift from ours?

You aggress, we respond. The shoreline shifts, the waters rise.

After the wave broke, I stayed close to your world. Your lab, the streets we walked, the movie theater—Wetworld had claimed them all.

But I could not bring myself to go far. My new cave is the room where you first saw me in human form, wedged behind rotting bookshelves whose contents dissolved long ago. Through them I can see the tank room, lined with cracked aquariums overgrown with algae. The adjacent exhibit hall, cracked movie screens warped and splintered, now houses to colonies of nudibranchs, and anemones squirm through the shattered glass.

The last time you sought me out, clad in your diving gear, your flesh looked like seaweed that had bleached in the sun. Behind your mask your lips moved, pleading. You reached out, but not as a caress.

My instincts flared. I shot past you, squeezed inside the cracked wall and remained there, just out of reach.

Tears leaked from your eyes, clouding your mask. We do not measure time as you do—yet much time seemed to have passed. You looked older, shrunken, a sag in your shoulders I had not seen before. Our eyes met, and you spoke the last human word I would ever hear. Remember.

You ascended to the surface, a long way upward. When your form parted the waters, I caught a glimpse of sunlight. For a brief second, I remembered all that had happened, all we had meant to one another.

I almost streaked through the water after you, to explain that I had no choice. Wetworld must always choose survival. Mercy is not a concept we can envelop. It is as foreign to our being as water is to air.

And then I shiver, the same shiver I felt when you touched me for the first time, my love, and shrink back into myself. Watching. Waiting. But for what I do not know.

About the Author

Empty-nester Michele Emmy lives in Colorado with her husband of 35 years. They have two grown children and one baby grandson, but are sadly out of pets at the moment. A former marine biology major, Michele remembers the resident octopus disappearing for days at a time, to be found skulking in a nearby tank.

A Clarion graduate and Colorado Gold fantasy award winner, Michele deals with the constant images and phrases popping into her head by grabbing her laptop and tapping them onto the page, where they belong. When not wrestling with imaginary creatures, she can be found messing with her five Instant Pots.

About the Publisher

ArmLin House is a unique publisher and production company. We help you develop your story in a memoir, business book, instructional video, and more. Then we format your story and help you present your work, whether you release it yourself or we do it for you. And once your story is out there, we can help you promote it with written and visual aids.

It's our mission to help our clients succeed in whatever they do. We take your visions and make them possible through coaching and distribution assistance. The products we produce are informational and entertaining. We also help clients market themselves and their businesses. We produce based on your needs, whether it be in print, digital, audio, or video formats. Then we help release it to a worldwide audience.

More About the Publisher

armlinhouse.com

www.ingramcontent.com/pod-product-compliance
Lightning Source LLC
Chambersburg PA
CBHW071948190726
48293CB00004B/1402